NOAH'S GOLD

Also by Frank Cottrell-Boyce

Millions
Framed
Cosmic
The Astounding Broccoli Boy
Sputnik's Guide to Life on Earth
The Great Rocket Robbery (World Book Day 2019)
Runaway Robot

Chitty Chitty Bang Bang Flies Again
Chitty Chitty Bang Bang and the Race Against Time
Chitty Chitty Bang Bang Over the Moon

FRANK COTTRELL-BOYCE

Illustrated by Steven Lenton

MACMILLAN CHILDREN'S BOOKS

Published 2021 by Macmillan Children's Books
an imprint of Pan Macmillan
The Smithson, 6 Briset Street, London EC1M 5NR
EU representative: Macmillan Publishers Ireland Ltd, 1st Floor,
The Liffey Trust Centre, 117–126 Sheriff Street Upper,
Dublin 1, D01 YC43
Associated companies throughout the world
www.panmacmillan.com

ISBN 978-1-5290-4826-1

Text copyright © Frank Cottrell-Boyce 2021
Illustrations copyright © Steven Lenton 2021

3 5 7 9 8 6 4

A CIP catalogue record for this book is available from the British Library.

Printed and bound by CPI Group (UK) Ltd, Croydon CR0 4YY

To my grandmothers

Sarah Grimes and Elizabeth Boyce

*And to all grandmothers – powering the future
by plugging it into the past.*

Dear Noah,

Just to be clear, you cannot carry on living on that island eating nothing but rabbits and blackberries. You need to get on and fix the internet.

You broke it.

You fix it.

When it's fixed, then we can come and get you. Not before - because until then, there's no buses, no trains, no boats and no petrol. Although - in case you've forgotten - we don't have a car any more.

We can't save you until you've saved us all.

Regards,

Mum and Dad

Noah Moriarty created WeeWord group **NOAH'S GOLD**
Noah added Eve to the group

Eve
Why is this called Noah's Gold . . . ?

Noah
Just thinking about Our Island . . .

Eve
And??

Noah
All the letters from when we were bus-wrecked.
I've tied them in bundles and put them under your
duvet. Read them again. Don't let anyone else read
them. Not yet. Because . . . Well, just read them.

Eve
And don't forget the map, plus
the recipe and police stuff . . .

Noah
Trust me. There's something
seriously rogue in there.

Eve
OK. Shall I read them now?
I'll read them now.

CONTENTS

ISLAND ~~of~~ ARANOR
Our Island

FRIDAY

⟜ BREAKFAST MENU ⟞

Choice of historic sandwiches:

Cheese & Rice Krispies

or

Peanut Butter & Grated Carrot

Letter 1

To: The Moriarty Family
35 Glenarm Terrace, Limavady

Dear Mum, Dad and Baby Isabella,

Good surprise finding that letter from you on the doorstep this morning! Thanks!

I didn't know they even had post on uninhabited islands! There is a postbox here, so I'll drop this letter in it when I've finished and see what happens. Not sure it'll work. Like everything else on the island, it looks like no one has used it for about a million years.

I've drawn you this map in case it comes in handy when you do come to rescue us, which I hope will be soon because, being honest, there's only so much Wild Food you can eat. Ryland Scally keeps mentioning that when people run out of food on uninhabited islands, they usually end up eating each other.

I'd like to avoid that if at all possible.

You sound upset about the internet being broken. I didn't break it on purpose! Being honest, I thought you wouldn't even mind. Dad, you're always saying people spend too much time looking at their screens and not enough time looking at the actual World. You're right there.

People definitely rely on their screens too much. For example, Mr Merriman relied on his satnav to take his Year Nine geography group to the Orinoco Wonder Warehouse in Letterkenny. That satnav did not take him where he wanted to go. It took him here, to an uninhabited island, which is a very, very different packet of crisps from a super storage and delivery depot.

For instance, the Wonder Warehouse is located in the historic market town of Letterkenny (Tidiest Town in Ireland 2016), whereas this island is located in the sea.

Also the Wonder Warehouse is full of stuff – such as food, books, trampolines, sports equipment and everything you could wish for.

Whereas this island is full of rocks.

We were shipwrecked by satnav.

I'm not blaming Mr Merriman, by the way. This trip was not even his idea. He's a geography teacher. He wanted his geography field trip to go to somewhere Geographical – such as the Giant's Causeway or the Marble Arch Caves. Everything would be fine now if they had done that. But no. They voted for this.

And why did they vote for this? Because of our Eve, that's why. She campaigned, remember. She said that Giant's Causeway and Marble Arch Caves were nothing but rocks. Funny shaped rocks. But rocks.

To be fair, Dad, you did point out that rocks were central to the study of geography.

Eve said, 'So are the things that people build on top of the rocks. For instance, the Orinoco Wonder Warehouse. Do you want to know what's so good about a Super Storage and Delivery Depot? I'll tell you what's so good about it.'

(Have you noticed, by the way, that Eve is always asking questions and then answering them herself before you get a chance?)

'It's the biggest warehouse in the World. Probably in the solar system. It's the internet with a roof on. Anything you buy online – that's where they keep it. It's too big to walk around. The workers have little scooters to get around the shelves. It's a continent of desirable items. What could be more Geographical than that?! Also it's indoors, so it won't matter if it rains.'

This is how Eve gets people to do what she wants. She makes what she wants to do sound like the spiciest thing on the menu. She started a WeeWord group, which she called 'The Wonder Warehouse vs Some Rocks. You Decide'.

The Wonder Warehouse won.

*

It should take about an hour to drive to Letterkenny. There were two minibuses. Mr Merriman was driving the one we were in. Ms Gyngell was driving the one in front. She'd been to the Wonder Warehouse once already to do the Health and Safety.

Somewhere on the A2 Mr Merriman's minibus ended up in front. He said he didn't need to follow anyone because the satnav would tell him what to do. A few minutes later the satnav told him to turn off the A2 on to one of those lanes with hedges on either side.

Ms Gyngell's minibus did not turn off. It sailed past us with her waving and staring at us in surprise. Her brake lights went on as if she was going to wait for us. But Mr Merriman's satnav said, '*Continue straight ahead*' – so that's what we did. No one else seemed to have even noticed.

From where I was – in the luggage section behind the back seat – all you could see was arms wobbling about in the air, with phones glowing in their hands. All you could hear was the pop of lunchboxes as people broke into their snacks. All you could smell was sweet chilli, barbecue beef, and cheese and onion crisps.

I was tempted to open up Eve's lunchbox for a snack, but decided to take in the view through the back window. I could see lots of clouds and hedges. I did not see a fleet of Orinoco Wonder Warehouse lorries driving up and down the lane. The lane got narrower – with grass growing up through the tarmac in the middle. There was no way you could even fit one lorry down it.

I know I'm not in the top set for geography – or anything – but I do know that if you build a Wonder Warehouse that sends goods and gifts all over the country, you put it somewhere with excellent road access and not at the end of a bumpy narrow lane. But Mr Merriman's satnav kept saying, '*Continue straight ahead*' – so we continued. Straight ahead.

I thought it was a worry, but nobody else seemed bothered to notice.

Do you know Lola Casement? She's on the school council, and if you didn't know that already, she'll tell you within ten seconds of meeting her. Anyway, she was reading out a leaflet about Orinoco Storage and Distribution. '*Our technology,*' she said, '*is here to help you find your heart's desire. On our shelves you will find everything you've ever wanted, from a microfibre hypoallergenic cleaning cloth to a motorboat. Our food aisle is one of the Wonders of the World . . .*' They all got so excited about food and motorboats that they started singing the school song:

Everywhere we goooooo
People wanna know-ooooo
Who we are
So we tell them
We are St Anthony of Padua
The mighty, mighty Anthony of Padua
And if they can't hear us
We tell them all again . . .

Which they do – do tell them again, I mean. And again. For about a million verses. They didn't stop singing until we came to the end of the lane, where we hit a little beach with a jetty. There was a ferry boat waiting at the jetty – one of those flat ones that look like a raft with railings. There was a van parked on its deck with 'SkyHooks Facilities' printed on the side.

Mr Merriman's satnav was still going, '*Continue straight ahead.*'

I thought, surely someone is going to shout, 'NO! Do not continue straight ahead! This is insane!' But no one did. I couldn't do it myself because I was hiding. I wasn't supposed to be there, but as things have turned out, it was a good job I was.

From,   Noah

PS Please send a helicopter or a boat when you can.

Letter 2

To: The Moriarty Family
35 Glenarm Terrace, Limavady

Dear Mum, Dad, etc.,

Sorry, I had to stop writing because it got dark and we have no electricity. Or candles.

I popped the other letter into the postbox, but I'm not sure it's going to work. How do letter boxes work? Should they make some kind of noise when you drop the letter in? Does the mail get sucked into a tube and shoot off to its destination? There was no sucking noise. Just a letter-dropping-into-a-hole sound. Then a bird flew out – which I don't think is a good sign.

There's a wee metal badge on the front of the postbox that says 'COLLECTIONS TUESDAYS, THURSDAYS AND SATURDAYS'. I don't know what collections are. and to be honest, we're not sure what day it is. I just wish I could text you, or WeeWord you or anything normal.

Anyways, Mr Merriman drove the minibus up the ramp and on to the back of this boat and parked it up next to the SkyHooks van. Right away a man with a beanie hat and hi-vis jacket jumped out of the van and waved at Mr Merriman to reverse.

Mr Merriman wound the window down and flapped some bits of paper at him, saying this was a geography field trip and he had all the permissions. The man didn't even look at the papers. He just pointed to the ramp and said, 'This is not a public ferry. Back up, please.'

The satnav said, '*Continue straight ahead.*'

Beanie Hat Man did not think this was funny.

Then another man – this one with very spiky hair – appeared from somewhere up at the pointy end of the boat, wanting to know why we hadn't left already. Then he spotted the minibus. 'Where,' he said, 'did you come from?' His voice was so deep it sounded like it was coming from inside an oven.

Mr Merriman explained about the geography trip.

Spiky Hair Man frowned. Then growled. But Beanie Hat Man smiled and told him to go and start up the engines. 'I'll take care of this,' he said. He looked inside the minibus. Everyone was taking selfies.

'How are we all doing for signal?' he said.

'Can't get any,' said Lola.

'Not so good out here, all right,' he said. He was wearing a badge that said 'PROUD TO BE A SKYHOOKS ENGINEER'. There was a blank bit at the top of the badge where his name should have been.

'You've picked a grand place for a geography field trip. Plenty of Geography on the island, all right. Big cliffs on the far side. Nice shallow bay on this side. That's what brings us here. We look after the Midas Transatlantic Submarine Internet Cable, which comes in here all the way from America. The island folk say that on a clear day, you can see Hy-Brasil from the top of the hill there, but that's not Geography. That's folklore.' The walkie-talkie attached to his jacket crackled. 'Well, best be off,' he said. 'Have a grand day, and when you're done, we'll take you back to the mainland. Careful of the cliffs. Have you your sandwiches with you? There's no facilities over there.' He gave the door of the minibus a friendly pat as if it was a horse. Then he told Spiky Hair Man to start the engines.

And off we sailed.

At no point did Mr Merriman say, 'You've mentioned cliffs and a shallow bay, but not the biggest warehouse in the World. Are we definitely going the right way?' Maybe Mr Merriman was thinking, *This may not be the right way to the Wonder Warehouse, but it does sound like the right way to a lot of Geography.*

The only thing I could do was stay hidden in the luggage bit and enjoy the view. There's an upside to being the smallest in the school – you can actually get quite comfy in the luggage bit of a minibus if you are the same size as a backpack.

13

I passed the time trying to work out whose bag was whose. Ryland Scally's backpack was bulky and bulgy like a backpack version of Ryland Scally. There was one bag that had a girl's face on it. The girl had stars in her eyes, and the straps were two great curling strands of hair. It was kind of horrible if you thought about it – as though someone had beheaded a faerie queen and was carrying the head around by the hair, with a skull-full of books and sandwiches. That definitely belonged to Ada Adamski, who talked like she had the faeries on speed dial.

The view outside the window was blue – blue sea, blue sky and, in the distance, blue islands. As soon as we were out on the water, this blizzard of big white birds whirled around the boat then spiralled off into the sky. They started dive-bombing the water so fast and so hard, you'd think they'd been shot. Then they'd bob up again, like flying popcorn. It turns out that this is the way they catch fish. They dive-bomb their dinner.

Ryland Scally got overexcited about this. He kept shouting that we were being attacked by eagles, though he did not let his fear of eagles get in the way of his cramming salt 'n' vinegar crisps into his mouth. In case you don't know Ryland, he's the one who never looks up from his Nintendo Switch. Even on a school trip when you're not supposed to have your console with you. I don't know if he got special permission to bring his. Or if it's superglued to his hand. Everyone used to think he must be good at computers, because he spends so much time on them. But it turns out he spent all of that time endlessly playing one game – *DogFight Rock* (the story of six strangers locked in mortal combat over scarce resources on a remote island). When his Switch stopped working, did Ryland say, *Oh well, let's play a real-life game instead?* Did he pick flowers or go birdwatching? No. He threw rocks. He threw rocks AT rocks. Because it wasn't computers he was into.

It was fights.

Dario Fogarty said, 'The fact is, they can't be eagles, because eagles are peak predators. Peak predators hunt alone or in pairs, not in flocks.' Eve had told me about Dario. Apparently, if God needs to fact-check something, he gets Dario to do it. The fact is, Dario loves a fact, and so he starts almost every sentence with the phrase 'the fact is'.

After a while the boat turned round in the water and backed up to a little stone jetty. It see-sawed on the water like a rocking horse. 'An easy boat to drive,' growled Spiky Hair Man, as he tied a rope to the jetty. 'Not so easy to handle.' Then Beanie Hat Man backed the van off the ramp so Mr Merriman could move the minibus. Mr Merriman's satnav told us to '*Continue straight ahead*', so we continued straight ahead, and everyone but me continued staring at their phones. I thought, someone should be looking out of the window, then if we really had gone the wrong way, someone would know the way back. Even if that someone was the youngest and smallest and wasn't even supposed to be there.

I will put some of the landmarks on the map later. For instance:

∗ At the end of the jetty – a bent metal sign that said

> AUTHORIZED PERSONNEL ONLY

I thought that was a bad sign.

∗ A little shop. The sign on the door said

> I. *Watson-Gandy, Purveyor of Fine Goods.*
> CLOSED. FROM NOW ON

Another bad sign.

* Two cottages. No one home. Looked like no one had been home since the Ice Age.
* A narrow shed-shaped thing next to the postbox – a bit like a green-and-cream wardrobe but with loads of windows.

> **NO PEOPLE.**
> **NO CARS.**
> **NO BIKES.**

The road rose, steeper and steeper, narrower and narrower, and higher and higher. With my face against the back window, I felt like if I opened the minibus door, I'd fall straight into the sea miles below. It was just like the feeling you get when you're on a roller coaster and it's chugging slowly, slowly up to the highest bit and there's a knot in your stomach that's getting tighter and tighter because you know any minute now you're going to be plunged down the other side.

The minibus stopped so suddenly that everyone jerked forward. I jerked forward so much I got my head stuck in the gap between the two back seats. Everyone would have seen me if they hadn't been looking at their phones.

'Something confusing has happened,' Mr Merriman said. 'Please wait here while I go and sort it out.

Won't be long. Nothing to worry about.'

I have never seen anyone look so worried as he looked when he said that bit about nothing to worry about. The minibus bounced a bit when he stepped down off it. The sound of seagulls breezed in through the open door. 'Do NOT move,' he said over his shoulder.

We didn't move.

But the minibus did.

Not much. But enough to make everyone scream like they were on a roller coaster.

I thought this was probably the moment to emerge from my hiding place and let people know I was there. So I shouted, 'Eve! Surprise!' But she wasn't there. Everyone had jumped off the minibus.

I tried to get out the back door, but it was locked. I was trapped and no one even knew I was there. I tried scrambling over the back seat, but someone grabbed my foot and pulled me. Eve had opened the back doors from the outside and was dragging me off the minibus. I tumbled out on top of her, and we both ended up on the grass. The air smelt salty and fresh. I took a big lungful the way you might swallow a big glug of water on a hot day.

When I looked up, the minibus was rolling away. I didn't understand exactly what was happening, but I did manage to snatch Eve's backpack out of the boot and hold it up over my head going, 'It's all right – I got it!'

Eve looked straight through me.

I was about to say, 'Who stole the jam from YOUR doughnut?' But then I followed her gaze. She was looking at the sea. Hundreds of feet below us. We were on top of a cliff.

It's strange, but the first thing I noticed was the white backs of the birds as they cruised across the calm, blue endless sea below. I say it was strange, because the birds and the sea were not the most interesting things to look at just then.

The really interesting thing at that moment was the minibus.

It was rolling towards the edge of the cliff.

And then suddenly it vanished.

I'm saying 'suddenly' because I can't think of another word to describe how quickly it happened.

You might think you know what suddenly means, but you haven't seen suddenly until you've seen your school minibus tip back and cartwheel off the edge of a cliff. It's the kind of suddenly that is so sudden you don't get time to believe what you're seeing.

There was a minibus.

Then no minibus.

Then a sound like a half a ton of pots and pans falling off a shelf.

Finally my brain said – *The minibus has fallen off a massive cliff.*

And we just got off it in time.

So anyways, I just thought you'd like to know that we didn't die yet.

From,

Noah

Letter 3

To: Mum and Dad
35 Glenarm Terrace, Limavady

Dear Mum, Dad (and Granny),

I didn't write the whole story in the last letter. I thought someone would've come to rescue us by now. But nothing yet. As I said, we're not dead. Though Ryland did accuse Mr Merriman of trying to kill us.

Mr Merriman was dazed. He kept saying, 'The satnav said straight on – the satnav said straight on . . .' Over and over. He looked into the blue sky maybe thinking if he looked hard enough, he might be able to spot the satellites whose advice he'd been taking and ask them what they were playing at.

Lola said, 'Are we there yet?' As though almost plunging to your doom over a cliff might have been part of the official itinerary. Everyone stared at her. 'I mean, we must be nearly there. We've been driving for hours.'

'Are we where?' said Eve, before answering herself. 'The Wonder Warehouse? No, we're not in a warehouse in Letterkenny. We are on the edge of a cliff, one nanometre from death. What are we going to do now?'

Lola looked like she was going to answer Eve's question, but Eve answered it herself. 'First,' she said, 'we make sure we are all here.'

'Yes!' said Mr Merriman. 'Counting heads. That's what we do.'

The point of counting heads is to make sure you've got all the kids you came out with and haven't lost one. So Mr Merriman was surprised to find that he not only had all the kids he set out with. He had an extra one too.

'How can there be six of you? There were only five when we left school.'

I put my hand up and explained that I was the extra child.

You're probably wondering what exactly I was doing on my big sister's geography field trip too. Partly, I was sort of kidnapped, but mostly it was because of the sandwiches.

You know, Eve got me so excited about this trip I kept asking her questions about it, including what she was having for lunch.

If you're off on a proper day out, then you should take a proper packed lunch. A decent pack of sandwiches in your bag makes the World your Happy Meal. You've

22

As she swung it over her shoulder, I could see the words 'NEEDED ON JOURNEY' written in big letters on a label tied to the strap. And I know this sounds mad, but I felt like that label was a message to me. Like *I* was needed on this trip. Because something huge was going to happen, and I was going to be part of it.

I was right about that first part anyway.

From,

Noah

Letter 4

Hi, Mum and ~~Dad~~ (also Granny),

I'm sure you're glad to hear I'm with Eve.

Although she's not exactly being sisterly.

I honestly thought our Eve would be pleased to see me.

She wasn't. She barely even looked at me. Everyone else did though. Ryland said I'd just appeared from nowhere. Ada said, 'He must live on the island. Are you a magical child?'

At home you can usually get Eve's attention by saying something outrageous so that she'll look up from her phone to correct you. So I said, 'That's me. Magical,' and gave a little bow.

Even then Eve didn't say anything.

Dario asked why a magical child would be wearing school uniform.

'All part of my magic,' I said.

Ada said, 'I'm sure he's magical. Look how small he is. He's like a wee hobbit.'

Hobbit?! I gave Eve a pleading look, but she just changed the subject.

'Will I tell you what I think has happened, Sir?' she said. 'When you put Orinoco into the satnav, maybe you forgot to add Wonder Warehouse, Letterkenny. So your satnav wasn't taking us to the warehouse. It was taking us to a giant river in South America. If the satnav thought we were going to South America, it would just keep heading west until it ran out of west. And this is where the west runs out, as far as Europe is concerned. We are now at the edge of the World.'

I thought Mr Merriman would be interested in this, with it being Geography. But he just stared at the sea.

Thinking that maybe he hadn't really understood, I said, 'The satnav was trying to get you to drive us to the actual Orinoco River. But that can't be done because there's about a million miles of water between here and Brazil.'

Mr Merriman stared at me. Then he stared at the sea. Then he stared at his phone. 'I . . .' he began. Then he stared at me again. Then he stared at the sea again. Then he said, 'I . . .' again. He seemed to be thinking that the sea was my fault.

'The fact is,' fact-checked Dario, 'it's not a million miles. It's only about five thousand miles to Brazil from here.'

Eve pointed out that five thousand miles is still a

long way. Especially over water in a minibus.

Everyone looked at Mr Merriman, expecting him to come up with a plan. Funny how you expect a grown-up to have a plan, even if that very grown-up has just nearly driven you off a cliff. Mr Merriman didn't have a plan. Unless the plan was to keep staring at the sea until it went away.

Ada remembered that the man on the boat had said you could see Brazil from here.

'That's not *Brazil*, Brazil,' said Dario. 'That's a different Brazil. *Hy-Brasil* – is a mythical, mystical mist-covered island, which can't be seen except for one day every seven years when the mist lifts. It's a myth and therefore can't be reached by actual boat.'

'So that's why there's a magical child here,' said Ada.

Eve said, 'Did the man on the boat say he'd take us home? He did. So will we go down to the jetty? We shall.'

Mr Merriman looked as though he'd been given the answer book to the World's hardest exam. 'The jetty!' he said. 'Let's go! Now which way?' He looked down at his phone. 'Does anyone have signal?'

No one had signal.

'How are we going to find the way back to the jetty?' said Ryland. 'If we've got no signal?'

'I'm sure there must be signal somewhere,' said Mr Merriman, and he wandered off up the hill to look for some.

Mad to think that just minutes after Mr Merriman's satnav nearly threw them off a cliff, they still trusted their phones to show them the way home.

Lola obviously thought we were in the kind of situation that called for her cheering-up skills. She said, 'Well it's bad that the minibus went over the cliff, but at least we weren't inside it. Is anybody hurt? Because I have the first-aid bag here if you've any cuts or bruises.' She was wearing the class first-aid bag round her neck like a Lady Mayoress's chain of office. No one had a cut or bruise. 'Yay! Go St Anthony's! And you know what? Just because it fell off a cliff, doesn't mean it's necessarily wrecked. Wait till we see. Maybe the minibus is just a wee bit scratched and we can all go home?'

As she said that, a thick cloud of oily black smoke floated up from under the edge of the cliff and hung in the air like a genie materializing from a lamp.

'Oh!' Ada gasped, pointing. 'Is that it? Is that Hy-Brasil? The mystical misty mythical island?'

'I think –' I coughed, the fumes from that smoke nearly choking me – 'that is probably the burning wreck of your minibus.'

Everyone went quiet again. Thinking about how

wrecked the minibus must be and how we were almost wrecked with it.

'We've got to see this,' said Ryland. He took a few steps towards the edge. Then stopped. 'Haven't we got to see this? I mean, the school minibus is on fire. You can't miss that. Come on.'

The others stepped towards him, but we all stopped well short of the edge. They wanted to see, but they didn't want to look.

'We could dangle him over the edge,' said Ryland, pointing at me. 'He's the lightest. We could hold him over the edge and he could take a picture.'

You could see that no one really wanted to do it. But also that no one really knew how to say no to the biggest boy in the class. He'd already grabbed hold of my arm with one hand. His other hand was still clutching his Switch.

'Where's Mr Merriman?' said Eve. Probably she was hoping that a teacher would stop this. But Ryland suddenly shook his Switch at us.

'Look!' he shrieked. 'Look what's happened!'

The screen had gone blank except for a message that said, EVERYTHING NOT SAVED WILL BE LOST.

'Lost –' Ada sighed – 'on a mythical island.'

'Don't worry,' said Eve, shoving me in front of her. 'The Hobbit will show us the way.'

32

It was harsh being called a hobbit by your own sister. She's different at school from the way she is at home, by the way. You know how at home she'd be making jokes and playing with Baby Isabella. Here she's the girl who knows what to do. People seemed to do exactly what she told them. Even Mr Merriman.

Actually, I did know the way back to the jetty. I'd been looking out of the window and not at my phone. To be honest, anyone who opened their eyes could tell you the way back. There were dirty great tracks in the grass where the minibus had driven over it. Plus, we were uphill, whereas the jetty was in the sea, which is always going to be downhill. So I set off down the slope with the others following me.

That felt good, by the way. The whole reason I'd jumped into the minibus was to save them from peanuts, and now here I was saving them from being lost. I felt exactly like what you said I was meant to be, Granny – a small person doing great deeds.

Lola tried to get the school song going again, but it didn't take off. Everyone was too busy checking their phones for signal. When we were well ahead of the others, Eve started on at me. 'What are you even doing here?'

'I thought you'd be pleased to see me.'

'You're not in my group,' she whispered. 'You're not even in my year. We're not even supposed to bring biscuits let alone little brothers.'

'Why aren't you allowed biscuits?'

'Biscuits are not the issue here. The issue is little brothers – you are here, where you're not supposed to be. And our minibus is also where it's not supposed to be, namely over a cliff – and are these two things connected?'

'I . . .'

'Did you touch the satnav?'

'No. Why would I touch the satnav?'

'The satnav went wrong,' said Eve, 'and nearly killed us, and I've a feeling you touched it.'

'But I didn't touch it.'

'What's that noise?'

For once Eve did not have an answer to her own question.

Ryland said it sounded like wolves.

'Fun fact,' said Dario. 'Wolves are shy, retiring animals, and you don't need to worry about them. Also it sounded nothing like wolves.'

Ada said that she wouldn't be surprised if it was faerie folk. Personally I think everyone – including Ada – would have been really very surprised if it was faerie folk.

It wasn't faerie folk. It was birds.

Beyond the wood was a huge knobbly outcrop of shiny white rock. 'A rock that makes a noise,' said Ada.

'Is it the door to the faeries' underground kingdom?'

I realized it was me she was asking. I looked at Eve and brazenly said something about the island magic.

The whole rock was covered in millions of those big white dive-bomber birds. They were like fat meringues, yattering away fit to deafen you.

'They're not faeries,' said Ryland. 'They're vultures.'

'The fact is,' said Dario, 'they're . . .'

Everyone looked at him, expecting a Dario fact-drop, but he was just staring at his phone.

'I don't know. I don't know what the fact is.' His eyes were brimming with sadness. 'I don't know anything. It was all in my phone, and now my phone doesn't work, I don't know anything. What are we going to do?! How are we going to know anything? There must be signal somewhere.'

'There'll be plenty of signal,' said Eve, 'when we get back to the mainland. Let's go to the jetty and get back on the boat. Come on.'

She pushed ahead of me and we picked up the pace.

The birds went quiet. They folded their wings. Turned their heads sideways, pretending not to look at us. But they were definitely looking at us. Sideways. The silence was intense.

Then . . . bird explosion.

Thousands of birds threw themselves into the sky. They poured over our heads. Their wings whisked the

35

air. We ducked. We ran downhill and didn't stop until we reached the wardrobe-shaped thing by the row of white cottages.

'That,' said Ada, 'was not comfortable.'

'Look!' whooped Lola, pointing at the row of white cottages. 'Aren't they cute? They're just like in that book *Katie Morag Delivers the Mail*. I love that book!'

It was just like Katie Morag, if there was a Katie Morag story in which Katie Morag delivered the mail in a tank and shot the letters through the letter boxes with high explosives. Their thatched roofs were shattered. Their doors battered and splintered. Long grass grew in all the gutters. Moss grew on the windowsills.

It made you wonder where the people had gone and why. As if something bad must have happened here once upon a long time ago.

'Sir,' said Ada, 'did something bad happen here once upon a time, d'you think?'

Everyone looked to see what Mr Merriman would say, but what we actually saw was that he had vanished. There was no sign of him.

Where did we lose him? In the woods? Had he been eaten by wolves? Taken away by the faeries? Dive-bombed by birds?

'He probably wandered off when we were looking for signal,' said Eve. 'He'll catch up. He knows we're going to the jetty. There it is.'

Lola began shouting, 'Yay! We did it! We found the jetty! Team St Anthony's, give yourselves a pat on the back.'

Ada said, 'It was the magic child – he led us here.'

I said, 'No problem. All part of the old magic.'

But there was a problem.

The jetty was there all right, exactly where I expected it to be. What was not there was the boat. The boat – our only way of getting home – had gone.

When I say gone, I don't mean vanished. When a thing is vanished, there's always a chance you're just

looking in the wrong place. We could see the boat all right, steaming away from us, scribbling smoke across the sky. A woman with a great cloud of fiery red hair was standing on the deck. She had not been there on the way over. A bright light was attached to the back of the boat, and the white of the SkyHooks van really stood out against the blue of the distant hills as it chugged off towards the mainland.

And away from us.

From,

Noah

Letter 5

To: Mum and Dad
35 Glenarm Terrace, Limavady

Mum, Dad (and Granny),

Hi. Me again. Sorry, had to stop writing for a while there to take my turn watching the fire. It wasn't easy to get the fire going. There's a story about that. I'll tell you now. I have loads of time to write these letters because hardly anyone talks to me, even our Eve, who is still acting like she's never seen me before in her life.

When we saw the boat leaving, we all ran out on to the jetty waving and shouting – but the boat did not turn round. It made no sense. Beanie Hat Man had promised to take us home.

The others weren't worried yet. They seemed sure that Mr Merriman would turn up, and off we'd go to the Wonder Warehouse.

I wandered off along the beach while they took selfies, or photos of shells and stuff. Over on the mainland, I could see tiny pinpricks of light strung out like faerie lights along the harbour. Somehow the lights made it look even further away.

It's ages since we've been on a beach together. I

think the last time was at Portrush when we were in that caravan?

This beach is different. It's just a little bay with walls of rocks at either end that look black at first, but when you get up close are loads of colours, because there's red seaweed spread over them, and rock pools with starfish in, and pink flowers growing in the cliff crevices. You'd like it.

On the far side of the jetty, there was a rusty metal sign that said 'FERRY TIMETABLE'. But all the times had been painted out and a laminated notice was tagged to the bottom that said, 'THE FERRY SERVICE FROM THIS ISLAND IS DISCONTINUED AS OF 17 MARCH 2004'.

I hadn't really thought about ferries, until I saw that there wasn't one.

There was another metal sign just beside the jetty. That one said 'CAUTION! BURIED STRUCTURE'. I thought that sounded interesting, so I had a little poke about in the sand. About a foot down, I found this thick bright yellow tube. It was hissing like a huge snake. I thought at first it really was a snake.

I dug around for a while more and found another one. This one was blue and it was making a noise too, more of a buzzing than a hiss. Well, it *was* . . . until I touched it. Then it stopped – just for a moment.

I had a bad feeling about that right away.

I tried to push the sand back into the hole as quick as I could. I noticed that further up the jetty, the buzzing tubes came up out of the sand and into a kind of grey metal cabinet.

Ada had taken her shoes off so she could paddle in the surf.

Lola wanted everyone lined up along the jetty for a team photo. Everyone except me. 'You're not in our team,' she said. 'So you can take the photo.' She wanted Mr Merriman in the photo, but there was still no sign of him. 'Do you think he's gone off in the boat?' she said. 'Maybe he's gone to get another minibus.'

She told me I needed to get somewhere higher up, because the perfect photo is all about the perfect angle. So I climbed up on top of that metal cabinet. I could feel it vibrating under my shoes.

You know the way you always joke about and call me Doctor Icicle because every time I touch the TV remote, the TV goes wrong? And you never let me do the self-checkout in Lidl, or play on the iPad because they glitch up the minute I touch them? Well, as I went to take the picture, Lola's phone froze.

Lola said not to worry and told Eve to give me her phone.

'No!' said Eve. 'Don't let him touch any more phones.'

Everyone looked at her.

Dario said, 'Harsh.'

Ada said, 'He's just a lost little boy. You don't even know him.'

You would think at this point Eve would say, *Yes I do – he's my little brother*. But no. She just said, 'That's why I'm not giving him my phone.'

I was about to say, *That's no way to*

talk about your little brother, but Ada put her phone in my hand, and when I looked down, it had frozen. She gave a little shocked squeal.

Ryland said if people didn't stop giving me phones, we'd be stuck on the island forever because I must be jinxed.

'No, no,' said Lola. 'Mr Merriman gave us all an information sheet for this trip, and in the top right-hand corner – look – a number to call in case of emergencies. So we'll call that number and someone will come and get us. Now let's all be radiators instead of drains and just stay happy. Have any of you any signal?'

No one had a signal.

They all began pacing up and down, looking at their phones again.

Ada restarted hers and held it like it was a kitten she was trying to coax to do a trick. Ryland kept shaking his. Maybe he was trying to scare it into finding a signal.

Lola asked me if I had any signal yet. I told her I didn't have a phone.

Ada guessed this was because magic and phones don't really go together.

Eve never said anything about it being a Moriarty family fact that a new phone would freeze like a Calippo the minute I opened the box.

Which is why I am the only Year Seven, probably in the whole World, who doesn't own a mobile phone. The only kid on earth who has never followed, shared or liked anything except In Real Life.

'If we can't find any signal,' said Ryland, 'how can we make an emergency phone call?'

'Logically,' said Dario, 'at least one of us should have signal because we're all on different networks. What's happened?'

As soon as he asked that, I thought I knew the answer.

I should have told them what happened while I went to take the team photograph. I should have told them what I saw on the mainland while they all had their backs to it, because they were smiling for the camera.

When Lola's phone froze in my hand, all the

twinkling lights on the mainland went out. If the harbour was a big birthday cake, someone had just blown out the candles. And underneath me, the buzzing from the metal cabinet stopped. As if the box, the lights, and me, and the phones were all connected. And the connection had broken.

That's when I remembered what the SkyHooks engineer had said about the Midas submarine internet cable landing on the island.

And I was thinking: *Did I just touch the actual internet?*

I'd broken the internet.

All I really, really wanted in the whole World just then was to tell a grown-up. But you're not here, Mum. And weirdly, neither was Mr Merriman. There was still no sign of him.

Ryland was shaking his phone harder than ever.

'We're trapped,' he said. 'Washed up. Like in *DogFight Rock*.'

No one knew what *DogFight Rock* was at that point. We've heard a lot about it since.

It's a game 'based on a true story' about some people who are marooned on an uninhabited island 'just like us'. In order to survive, they have to fight for scarce resources like food and water and shelter.

'Oh,' said Lola. 'But we don't know this island is

45

uninhabited. We've only seen a little corner of it. For all we know, there could be a Pizza Hut just behind that hill.'

Everyone stared up at the hill, trying to spot a Pizza Hut. But they could all see it wasn't really a Pizza Hut kind of hill.

'Why did you have to talk about food?' Ada sighed. 'I wasn't even a bit hungry till you said that, and now I'm starving.'

'Starving,' said Ryland, 'is how it all starts. First they get starving. Then they get eating each other.'

'Well they should've brought sandwiches,' said Lola. 'St Anthony's brought sandwiches, didn't we, St Anthony's? Yay!'

They all realized the truth at the same time.

'I don't know about you,' said Dario, 'but I . . .'

'Left them on the bus,' said everyone except me.

'Our sandwiches,' said Eve, 'are toast.'

'The fact is,' said Dario, 'they're more likely to be flame-grilled than toasted. Given the fact that the van exploded.'

I grabbed Eve's bag.

She absolutely barked at me, 'Don't touch my bag!'

But when I pulled the huge foil-wrapped doorstep of historic sandwiches out, she went quiet, and so did everyone else.

Even though we had just survived a bus crash, and

were now shipwrecked on an uninhabited island, and I may possibly have destroyed the internet, I still had room in my head to be excited to see what people would think about them. I undid the foil, spread it on a big rock, stepped back and said, 'There. Work away.'

I remember another one of your sayings, Granny: '*Life is a party. Don't show up with one arm as long as the other. Bring something to the party*.' Definitely I was bringing something to this party. It made me feel a bit better about destroying the internet.

'Oh, and stand back,' I said, 'if you've got nut allergies.'

No one stood back.

Everyone stared.

'Eve! All that's your packed lunch?!' Lola gasped. 'Or were you planning to feed the World?'

'You had all those sandwiches and you tried to keep them secret, even though you knew we were starving?' said Ryland. 'That's exactly what I'm talking about.

Not to brag, but I thought you'd like to hear some of the things they said about those sandwiches:

> 'A sandwich that bites back when you bite it.'
> – Dario

(Which was exactly the reaction I was hoping for.)

> 'Why does he (that's me by the way) get to share your sandwiches? He's not in our group or anything. Our resources are limited. We shouldn't share them with strangers.'
> – Ryland

Eve still didn't stick up for me. But she did pass me some of her sandwiches when no one was looking. I've seen you do that, Mum, to Baby Isabella, when we've been a bit short of food at home.

Until we'd eaten, the island

Dario went off to look in all the rock pools. Ada paddled in the waves. Lola lay out on the sand sunbathing.

'Team St Anthony's,' she said, 'is having a picnic at the seaside. What is not to like?'

Everyone looked so cheerful and chilled. Their school blazers were in a pile on the rocks. They'd all rolled up their shirt sleeves and trouser legs as if this was just another day at the seaside.

But my head was buzzing.

Some people are allergic to nuts. Could it be that some gadgets are allergic to me? *Had* I just broken the actual internet?

I was trying to think about some of the things that you'd said, Dad, about how the World turned just as quickly before mobile phones were invented. So how did they rescue people before mobile phones?

That's when I remembered what the cream-and-green wardrobey thing with all the tiny windows was. As soon as I thought of it, I ran over to it. The others must have thought something was happening. They all ran from the time before proper phones were invented.'

See, this was why I was 'NEEDED ON JOURNEY' – because, thanks to me, in one phone call, I'd have us out of here. Possibly in a helicopter. I was already feeling like a proper hero.

You probably remember using phone boxes like this in the olden days, Dad, but we'd never seen one for real. The phone doesn't even look like a phone. It looks more like a black cat dangling its curly black tail down the side of a big metal box. The face of the cat is a metal dial with holes in. There's numbers in the holes.

Everyone reached for their phones so as to google how to use an old-fashioned phone, forgetting that the reason they needed to use an old-fashioned phone was that their proper phones didn't work.

'We'll figure it out,' said Eve. 'Then we'll call the coastguard. They've got boats. They've got helicopters. All we need is the coastguard number.'

Again everyone reached for their own phones to

It took a while to work that out. At first we were putting our fingers in the holes and pushing the numbers. Eventually Eve remembered seeing it done in a movie. She dialled the number, then lifted up the handset. It purred like a cat. But nothing happened.

'Maybe,' said Dario, 'you pick up the handset bit first and then dial.'

Eve tried holding the handset bit, and then dialling. But she'd only dialled one number when the purr changed to a cat wail. She slammed the phone down. Then Eve picked it up again. It was purring.

'Well, it didn't like that.'

A lot of people had ideas about what the phone might like. They all shouted them at once.

'Dial first.'

'Pick up first.'

'Pick up.'

'Put down.'

'What about the numbers written across the middle of the dial? Could they be something?'

writing said '50c MIN'. Eve asked if we thought it was a code.

'*Min* is minimum, and the *fifty* must be fifty cents. Minimum payment. Fifty cents?' said Ada. When everyone looked to see what she was on about, she said, 'You had to pay to use phones back in the day. This is a pay-as-you-go phone that doesn't go anywhere. There's one in *Paddington 2* when he escapes from jail—'

'Of course!' interrupted Eve. 'Who's got fifty cents?'

No one had fifty cents. No one had any coins at all. We searched our pockets, searched the ground. Nothing.

Eve let the door swing shut behind her.

Everyone looked away towards the mainland. It seemed even further away than it did before.

It feels like we've been here days and days. Eve is still acting like I'm invisible. Home seems long ago. Please write back.

Obviously no one had matches.

Lola said not to worry, people all over the World were starting fires without matches all the time. For instance with magnifying glasses. All you needed was a magnifying glass to concentrate the rays of the sun.

No one had brought a magnifying glass. We were on a trip to see the biggest warehouse in the World. We were confident it would be visible to the naked eye.

Dario said that people were lighting fires long before magnifying glasses were invented. 'We just need to find out how. Let's look it up, shall we?'

'Look it up where?' asked Eve.

'Oh,' said Dario.

Dario was definitely the one who was missing his phone the most.

Eve said, 'How do you light the fire in *DogFight Rock*, Ryland?'

'From a volcano.'

People did not look convinced that this was a good idea. We had a quick look round. There was not a sniff of volcano to be seen anywhere. Volcanic fire-lighting was not an option.

Lola passed round a little mirror, saying she was sure that mirrors could somehow set fire to things, but she couldn't remember how. Ada used it to make little flashes of light skitter over the sand – 'Like faeries,' she said, smiling at me, as if that was something I'd really like. 'I'm sure the magic child can light a fire,' she said.

Actually, I did remember something about lighting fires.

Remember when Eve went on that Outward Bound thing in Cushendall? She went on forever about abseiling and outdoor cooking and how she could tie special knots.

I said, 'My big sister showed me how to do it.' Thinking Eve would definitely finally admit to being my sister.

She said nothing.

Except when I said, 'I'll need something really dry.' She said, 'Obviously there's tons of that, this being a beach.' Really sarcastically.

Ada spotted a pile of old fishing nets under the trees. They were white where the sun had bleached them and dry as straw.

'I need a bottle of water,' I said.

'He's going to make fire out of water!' Ada gasped, handing me her official St Anthony of Padua High School drinking bottle.

'You fill the bottle with water, then use it like a magnifying glass to focus the sun on the bits of dried rope thread,' I said, and I held it as still as I could. For *ages* . . . Nothing was happening. 'You just have to be patient.'

But there was no time to be patient.

'I wonder,' said Eve, 'if there's a box of matches in the cottage.'

That's when Ryland yelled, 'Look! Over there!'

Only nobody looked over there at first because, when he shouted, he sprayed bits of salt 'n' vinegar crisps everywhere.

'Are you eating crisps?' said Lola. 'Have you been hiding a packet of crisps and not sharing them? That's not very nice. Where are you hiding them?'

Ryland said he wasn't hiding them. They were his crisps and anyway they were all gone now.

'Show us the packet.'

'There. Packet. Empty,' said Ryland, and he threw the packet on to the not-on-fire fire.

The packet floated down to where I was willing the fishing net to burst into flames. I said, 'There's loads of crisps in here.'

'Will you please forget the crisps and look!'

We looked where he was pointing. It was a plane. Flying low in the sky, towards the island. When I say low, I mean very low. Like, worrying low. It flattened the waves of the sea as it passed. It drowned all noise except its own. I don't know how low it was, but it was low enough to make us not want to sit there watching. We could see windows. We could see faces in windows.

'Come on, St Anthony's!' yelled Lola. 'Wave and shout!'

It didn't seem likely that the pilot would hear us over the sound of those engines. But Eve shouted, 'Phone torches!' They all shone their phone torches into the air. Ada flashed the little mirror at the plane.

When it was far away, we thought it was a little plane like the little red plane in *Peppa Pig*. As it got nearer and louder, we saw that it was not little at all. It was a grown-up plane, the kind that can swallow two hundred passengers and all their luggage. And it looked like it was going to crash.

We threw ourselves flat on the sand.

Then we got scared and ran. We all knew really that we probably couldn't outrun a plane, but none of us felt like sitting there to see what would happen if we didn't try. We tore up the hill, past the cottages.

We all flung ourselves down on the ground as it passed overhead.

The oily smell of the fuel made me feel dizzy. Afterwards I noticed that the white walls of the old cottages had black stuff all over them.

We all kept watching until it had cleared the top of the hill. It was only when it was gone that we realized we were all holding hands.

'Thank you, Jesus,' said Lola as soon as it was out of sight. 'Do you think it's going to crash?' We stood listening, wondering if there would be a huge splash or a plume of smoke.

Ada was worried that it was her fault. That she'd done it with the mirror. Everyone said no. All the same, Ada didn't look away from the horizon. Neither did the others.

After a while, the plane reappeared, much higher in the sky this time, and now it was turning in a wide circle, heading back towards the mainland.

'Yay! It didn't crash!' whooped Lola. 'I was so worried there was going to be explosions and stuff.'

'No,' said Dario. 'Not yay. Not even a little bit yay. A plane just nearly smashed into us, and now it's wandering round the sky like a lost puppy. What is going on?'

We walked back down to the beach. The fire had gone from being not-on-fire to a blazing, smoking proper bonfire.

Ada stared at me. 'How did he do that?' she cried.

'That,' said Ryland, 'is rogue.'

I just shrugged and said, 'Small bit of magic.' I thought that would outrage Eve into finally saying something, but no.

I knew how the fire started, by the way. It was the crisp packet. When you think about it, crisps are just cold chips, and as Granny Nuala says, '*A chip pan is basically waiting to burn your house down.*' My water-bottle-magnifying-glass trick must have finally made a spark. The gust of wind from the plane fanned it into flames. And the crisps were the fuel. So – hey presto – fire.

Worth remembering if you're stuck that a crisp packet is an absolutely rogue fire starter.

By the way, I didn't mention any of that to Ada.

Everyone stood warming themselves at the fire. Fire really does seem like magic. The way it turns cold into warmth and worry into cheer and – on that night – the only boat on the island into ashes.

Eve still didn't speak to me. She was looking towards a dot of light in the sky above the hills. We all thought it was another plane and got ready to run again. But after a while, we saw it wasn't moving.

Ryland said, 'Maybe it's parked?'

'Fun fact,' said Dario. 'You can't park a plane in the sky. If a plane stops flying, it falls down.'

'It's not a plane,' Eve pointed out. 'That,' she said, 'is the evening star.'

'Another fun fact,' said Dario. 'The evening star is not really a star. It's a planet.' He looked sad again. 'But I can't remember which planet.'

Lola was not happy about the evening star.

'EVENING star?' she said. 'You mean it's evening now. Where is Mr Merriman? Where is he? Where's he gone? Why is no one helping us? It's getting dark.'

Ada said maybe the reason Mr Merriman couldn't find us was that the island was in an alternative magical dimension. 'Like Hy-Brasil. Which would not be good.'

Lola asked her why it wouldn't be good.

'Well, what if we spend one night here and then go home and find out that a hundred years have passed since we went away and everyone we know is old or dead.'

This wasn't a thought that was going to help us get a good night's sleep.

From,

Noah

Letter 7

To: Mr Moriarty
35 Glenarm Terrace, Limavady

Dear Dad,

Guess what? I've got an actual address. Hopefully that will make it easier for you to write back. It's Sea View Cottage, Island of AranOr. At last we know where we are!

It happened like this . . .

Everyone had different ideas about ways we could get a good night's sleep.

Ryland's idea was – go home. Everyone said this was a great idea, and did he happen to have a helicopter or a boat, because that's all we'd need to get home? Sadly he didn't.

Dario said we could check out Airbnb or TripAdvisor. 'Just because we haven't seen any hotels or bed and breakfasts, doesn't mean there aren't any. We haven't seen the whole island.'

Everyone said this was also a great idea. But that to look up things up, you need a signal, which we didn't have.

I said, 'We could try a cottage.'

Everyone said nothing. It was as if my words had disappeared into the air.

I said again, 'How about one of the cottages?'

No one replied again.

Then Eve said, 'How about one of the cottages?' And everyone said this was a great idea.

The end cottage was the one that had the most roof. The paint was peeling from its door in big jagged flakes. The door was still in the doorway but kind of slumped. The hinges were crumbling into rust.

Lola wondered if we should knock – 'Just in case there's someone in.'

'If there's someone in,' said Eve, 'we don't want to meet them.'

The others laughed. She can be funny when she wants to be, and it makes other people feel a bit braver.

Eve was the first into the cottage. She didn't exactly open the door – more sort of moved it aside. The last light of the day poured in through the hole in the roof. The thing you most noticed was dust. There was a lot of dust. And spiders' webs.

The rickety table had a tablecloth of dust, and the spindly chairs around it had cushions of dust. There was a little wooden statue on the mantelpiece of a man with a bald head holding a baby.

'That's slightly rogue,' said Ryland. 'There's a statue of the same bloke outside our school.'

Eve pointed out that the bloke was St Anthony of Padua, and that our school was named after him.

'So what's he doing here?' said Ryland.

'Maybe his satnav went wrong too,' said Eve.

Lola said we'd get the place cleaned up in no time. 'We could take *before* and *after* pictures,' she said.

Ryland said there was no point in taking pictures when you couldn't put them up on your feed.

Lola said that we'd be home tomorrow probably, and everything would be back to normal and we'd have signal again.

Ryland shrugged. 'Sound.'

So that was decided, and Lola took photos of us all surrounded by dust and spiders' webs. Then she said, 'Let's do this.'

Water was the first problem. When Eve turned on the tap over the sink, it sputtered, spat some green stuff out, made a hideous noise, then stopped.

'The fact is,' said Dario, 'there's a sea full of water. And there's buckets.'

We found two buckets and two brooms hanging from hooks on the wall. There were more hooks, which turned out to be exactly right for hanging the spindly chairs from.

Eve said that they probably hung the chairs up when they were cleaning the floor. They must have been clean, organized people.

We did TRY to not think too much about them, but we kept finding distracting clues. For instance, there was a tin that said *Golden Syrup* on the outside, which turned out to contain some buttons, string and a key ring with one copper key and one silver key. Neither of them fitted the keyhole in the cottage door. And at the very bottom of the tin was some stamps! That's what made me remember that you need stamps to post a letter. I'm going to use one of them for this letter.

Dario found leaflets in an old sewing machine table – including one that said *Operation SkyHooks – In This Together.*

And there were brown envelopes with seeds inside. Someone had written on the front in big neat letters:

Sweet Peas – Plant in October. Wintering makes them stronger.
Cucumber Seeds – From Desi's cucumbers.
Beans – From our own crop.

'They never got round to planting these,' said Eve. 'So they must have left before October.'

'But not last October,' said Dario. 'Look at this.' There was a wedding photo in a frame.

Ryland said that the people in it must be dead because it was in black and white, and everyone from the black-and-white days is dead now.

To be fair, there was a little plastic card with a photo of an old woman on the front and a prayer for the repose of her soul on the back, so someone was dead. But there was also a box of Pictionary that didn't look too old.

We opened the drawers of the wobbly table and found a packet of envelopes tied with string. All the envelopes were stuffed full.

'They're letters,' Eve said. 'Before messaging days, people used to write their news down on bits of paper and post it into letter boxes and then the postman brought it to the door.'

The front of the envelopes said, 'E. McAlister, AranOr, Donegal'.

So that's how we know that this island is officially called AranOr.

I'll put that on the map later.

'You could almost imagine E. McAlister strolling back in,' said Ada.

'Makes you wonder why they walked out,' said Ryland.

Lola said that almost imagining people was not getting the floor clean. She sent me off to get seawater. She got Ryland brushing floors. The best part was when Dario looked in a little shed at the back and discovered that it was a toilet.

We all suddenly needed to go. Dario went first and it flushed, but after that it wouldn't flush again, which was embarrassing, until Eve thought of filling the cistern up using buckets of seawater. We found a big barrel and filled it up so the toilet would always be ready.

'Now,' said Lola, 'we are starting to get the place civilized.'

Civilizing the place was tiring, but also made you forget that you were bus-wrecked and forgotten in a World with no internet. By the time we'd finished, moonlight was pouring in through the hole in the roof and the cottage looked like a really nice place to live, except for the hole in the roof.

Ada wanted to read the letters. 'Then we'd know all about the people who lived here and maybe why they left.'

Lola said it was wrong to read other people's messages, even if the people were in black and white.

'Maybe we don't want to know why they left,' said Ryland. 'Maybe whatever got Mr Merriman, got them.'

Lola told him off for talking about scary things at bedtime. 'How can it be bedtime?' said Ryland. 'There are no beds.'

This was true, but Eve had an idea about that – probably the best idea in the history of the island. Remember how Ada found some fishing nets earlier? They were huge and squashy but dry. We dragged them up to the cottage and hung them from the hooks in the cottage wall.

'There you have it,' she said. 'Hammocks. One for boys, and one for girls.'

Ada said it was just like the dormitories in Harry Potter.

Ryland wanted the house to have a name. Obviously Ada suggested calling it Faerie Fireside or Pixie Parlour or something. Dario wanted to call it The Cottage, because, 'The fact is, it's a cottage.' Everyone thought Ryland would go for Fortress Ryland or Castle Destruction. But he said, 'I'd like to call it Sea View Cottage because it has a nice view of the sea.'

Lola said we'd need duvets to keep us warm. Surprisingly no one had brought a duvet with them on the school trip. Lola pointed out that there was a shop and why not try in there.

'Because the shop is shut?' said Dario. 'Like most shops on uninhabited islands.'

The shop windows were thick with dust and spiders' webs. We could just about see a rack of postcards with views of the island leaning against the glass.

It was definitely shut.

But the door was not locked.

There was a discussion about whether it was all right to go in or not. If you take things from an abandoned shop, is it still shoplifting?

We decided to go in and buy some duvets. Eve had a scrap of paper in her pocket and she wrote a note saying *We don't have any money at the minute. We will pay full price for the duvets as soon as our phones start working. Yours – St Anthony of Padua geography group.* And she put *To: I. Watson-Gandy Purveyor of Fine Goods* on the back. There was some debate about what the 'I' might stand for. But that was only because no one wanted to go into a shop full of spiders' webs in the dark. Ada said I should go first as I was protected by magic. I thought Eve might step in to protect me, but no.

When we opened the door, a bell rang. That made us all jump. Inside the shop there was that rack of postcards and . . . nothing else at all. Unless you count a little heap of bird poo in the corner.

I did take one of the postcards. I'll put it in the envelope with this letter.

It was strange to think that back in the day, people must have come here on their holidays. Otherwise why have postcards? But no one had bought one of these postcards for years. The sun had faded all the colours. It made you think of all the days when the sun had shone through these windows but no one had come through the door.

On the wall behind the counter there was a black-and-white photo of a woman with curly hair and overalls. Her eyebrow was raised as if she'd just caught you trying to steal a sweet from the pick-and-mix. That must be I. Watson-Gandy. I wondered if the 'I' stood

71

for Isabella, which made me really miss Baby Isabella.

Ryland was looking up at the photo too. 'Thanks,' he said, 'for nothing. Including no duvets.'

The bell over the door rang again when we left.

That night, I shared a hammock with Ryland and Dario, the three of us lying sideways. It was not that warm. The coldest bit was your feet. I suppose if we'd kept our shoes on, they might have been warmer but less comfortable. In the end we used our blazers to keep our feet warm.

'If we'd got to the Orinoco Wonder Warehouse,' said Dario, 'we could all grab a duvet from Aisle 83 North.'

When the others realized Dario was studying the map of the Wonder Warehouse that Mr Merriman had given out, they all did the same. Ryland noticed that there was an entire sector of games and consoles. 'There must be games in there I've never played,' he said. He made them sound like undiscovered planets.

Lola noticed that there were seven whole aisles of snacks and confectionery. 'That's about a mile of crisps and chocolate,' she said. 'Imagine.' Everyone went quiet while imagining a mile of crisps and chocolate.

The hole in the roof was full of stars. They did not

look like the normal stars we see at home. It looked like someone spray-painted the night with luminous caster sugar. I know it sounds mad, but I wondered if something had gone wrong with the sky as well as the phones. Maybe the luminous caster sugar was hundreds of satellites exploding into millions of pieces.

Dario read out the description of the Wonder Warehouse DIY zone. 'I wonder,' he said, 'if they sell anything that we could use to fix the roof?'

'The kitchen in the picture looks just like our kitchen at home,' said Ryland. He was clutching his Switch console to his chest like it was a teddy bear.

Everyone was talking about the Wonder Warehouse, but everyone was thinking of home.

They all had one last try of their phones, but still no one had any signal. Dario turned his off 'to conserve battery power', and the others did the same.

The moon had rolled into view in the hole in the roof. It looked like a massive cheese. When everyone went quiet, I whispered, 'Goodnight, Eve.' And I think she whispered, 'Goodnight, Noah,' like she would have at home, though that might have been the wind coming through the roof. Still, it made me feel as if in the morning everything would be normal again.

We'd wake up with the internet cabinet humming.

And even without a phone box or a phone signal,

it would still be OK because all we needed was the island's Wi-Fi to FaceTime our parents, and send an SOS to the coastguard, and – boom!

And if it isn't? Well.

Nearly everyone in History had no phone. People lived without the internet for hundreds of years, didn't they? As you are always reminding us, Dad. Granny was a grown-up before the internet was even invented.

Romans had no phones and they got stuff done. Vikings had no phones and they got about. Although you wouldn't want to share a boat with them.

The more I thought about History, the more History seemed to be mostly people burning things down and fighting and feeling hungry.

Before phones, no one had enough to eat. *After phones*, you just spoke into Siri or whatever, and the next thing – ABRACADABRA – there's a pizza at your door.

A phone is like a genie, ready to fulfil your every command. You can ask it pretty much anything. For example, you can ask it to tell your mum and dad exactly where you are so they can come and get you.

Before Phone History is men in top hats shoving children up chimneys. Or men in togas feeding each other to lions. *Before Phone History* is people writing letters to each other, hoping that somehow they will get them. Instead of sending a message, or making a phone call and hearing a real voice. History is lonely and frightening. That's why I'm writing these letters to you.

From,

Noah

PS Don't forget to write back. I miss you all.

TO: Noah
Sea View Cottage, AranOr

Dear Noah,

Hope this letter reaches you. We're really pleased to hear that you're alive. Yay!

You're in a ton of trouble for stowing away on your big sister's geography trip though.

First – Yes, you *do* have to put stamps on an envelope before anyone can reply to it.

Second – What are you even doing on an uninhabited island in the middle of the sea?!

You're supposed to be at school. You know Granny's saying about people being in the wrong place? 'If you find yourself wanting to wander off into the forest, that might be because the wolves have been praying for lunch.' You don't want to be the answer to a wolf's prayer.

So, you think you only broke the internet for Ireland?

No. NO. You broke it for the whole of Europe.

Maybe the World. We don't know, because we don't get news any more.

Did you not remember electronics are basically allergic to you?

We all know phones freeze when you pick them up. There was the terrible incident with the microwave. We try not to talk about that, but that does not mean we've forgotten about it. You also have a bad effect on the TV remote control. And the central heating.

Maybe you think the company that looks after the internet – SkyHooks or whatever – is going to come to the island and fix it? Maybe they will, but everyone's a bit busy right now. Schools, hospitals, traffic lights – none of them is working. It's chaos.

When people hear bad news, they always look for someone to blame. In this case they will blame you. Because it is basically all your fault.

And about Eve not talking to you . . . what do you want her to say?

'Hi, everyone. This is my little brother. He just killed your internet'?

Best keep quiet. Because if this was a Marvel film, you would be the biggest, baddest villain in the universe. You make the Joker look like Postman Pat.

Look, Noah, what do we do at home when the internet doesn't work? We go to the internet box and we turn it off and then turn it on again.

Always works.

Somewhere on the island there is an internet box. Just like ours, only a bit bigger and slightly more important. It's likely to be in a building to keep it safe.

Go in and find the reset button and turn the internet off and turn it on again.

Sincerely, etc.

Mum, Dad etc.

PS Remember no one is coming to rescue you. Including the people who sailed away from the island. They definitely saw the burning wreck of the minibus. So they think you're dead. If Mr Merriman was with them, he thinks you're dead too.

PPS Do NOT mention this letter to the other kids. People – especially kids – do terrible things when they are frightened or hungry. The best thing you can do is cook, which is the thing you are actually good at. As Granny once said, 'No one ever went on a murderous killing spree after a nice meal.' Let's not think how she knows this.

SATURDAY MORNING

SECOND BREAKFAST MENU

Chef's Special:
Neither Green nor Curry
or
No Breakfast

Letter 1

To: Everyone @ Glenarm Terrace etc

Mum, Dad and Everyone,

I'm glad I was up before everyone else so that I was the first to find your letter by the door. How do they get here – that's what I'm wondering? Does a drone drop them off or something? Does the postie bring them? If he does, he must come in a boat, so he could maybe rescue us. This morning I tried to see if I could catch him, but when I got outside – and this is really true – the whole island had disappeared.

Also the sea.

Being honest, I could hear the sea, but I couldn't see it.

Couldn't see my own feet even.

Everything was blurred. The ground was covered in mist as though someone had wrapped it in tissue paper. It was so misty it made you think Ada might be right. Maybe this is a mystical magical island. Maybe the government thought the very best place to put the Midas Transatlantic Submarine Internet Cable would be a magical island, because that's where it would be safe from sabotage and vandals and from people it's allergic to – such as me. It was also cold and wet. I wished I had something warmer than my school blazer to wear.

But I know you're right about how if this was my fault, I should fix it.

I honestly thought I could fix it before the others woke up. I thought all I had to do was stroll down to the jetty, to that metal cabinet with the wires going into it. Have a look inside to see if there was a reset button. Turn it off and turn it on again. Then I'd stroll back into the cottage and say, 'TA-DA! I just fixed the internet and saved the World,' and Eve would be like, 'That's my brother, that is.'

It was true. No one was coming to rescue us, but we could rescue everyone else.

I had to get to the jetty. Except I couldn't actually *see* the jetty.

I knew it was in the sea, so I tried to follow the sound of the waves. Except, the sound of the waves seemed to be coming from all around me. The more I tried to follow it, the more lost I felt. Then I heard a noise a bit like the spooky giggle you get in a faerie story just before the hobgoblin grabs you. But it also sounded like a toilet being flushed – which is not a sound they have in faerieland.

A few seconds later, my feet were wet and I realized the noise was being made by a stream, which I'd just sloshed through in my school shoes.

Then I heard a noise. Someone or something was slushing through the water behind me. Its wet feet flipped on to the pebbles. Nearer and nearer it came. I tried to run, but it snatched at my arm, trying to pull me back with long, scratchy fingers. And now the feet seemed to be ahead of me. And to the side. And to the other side. I was surrounded by unknown squelchy creatures lurking in the mist.

I turned round and a huge shape billowed up in front of me – a human shape made of mist, churning and changing as it came at me. It swelled up to giant size, shrank, rose up again.

All at once, the mist glowed red. Like the whole World was on fire. I'd never seen anything more beautiful or more frightening. Then something tore a hole in it and I could see rocks and grass.

Another hole, and there was the sea and the jetty. But they were miles below me. I must have been walking uphill for ages without noticing. I could now see that I was right up by the big rock where the dive-bomber birds hung out.

Another tear in the mist and I could see spiky bushes. *That's* what scratched me on the way up! The sun had come out. It was warming the mist and peeling the tissue wrapper off the World like it was a present. The sun tore away another strip and guess what was underneath?

The biggest chicken nugget in the bucket, that's what.

Ryland.

He was standing at the end of the rock. Right at the very edge of the drop. One step back and he'd fall into the sea below.

He said, 'What are you up to, up here on your own?'

I said, 'Ryland! Take a step towards me.'

'Don't tell me what to do! You're not the boss of me.'

I swear he was going to step back over the cliff just to prove his point.

I explained that I was trying to save his life and all he had to do was walk towards me.

'NOW! RYLAND!'

I said it so loud that he almost jumped forward. Dozens of birds flocked into the air and wheeled around the rock.

Ryland looked back over his shoulder. I couldn't see his face, but I did see his shoulders sway as if he was going to faint. Then he turned round and snarled, 'I asked you what you were doing up here. Who even are you?'

I was impressed that he got his angry face back on so quickly after almost walking off a cliff. I said, 'Eggs!

For breakfast. That's what I'm doing up here. Looking for eggs.'

His head swivelled with excitement. 'Is there a shop?' he said.

'No, but there are birds.'

'Eggs come from chickens, not vultures.'

'These aren't vultures.'

'They're not chickens either.'

'But they do lay eggs. So what's the difference?'

It turns out there is a massive difference.

If you are a chicken, laying eggs for someone's breakfast is a job. The farmer feeds you. You lay eggs. Taking an egg off a chicken is more or less the same as walking into a shop and taking something off a shelf. The chicken says, *Yes, no problem. Would you like a packet of salt 'n' vinegar crisps too?*

Taking an egg off a big dive-bomber bird was more like bursting into someone's bedroom and demanding to eat their children. When it comes to making breakfast, a packet of Weetabix is a lot more convenient.

When we took a step towards them, the birds put their heads back and opened their beaks. The sound that came out was like a car park full of faulty car alarms.

'Look!' yelled Ryland, his eyes wide with fear. 'They're getting bigger!'

'I think that's because we are walking towards them.'

Back home, if you just sneeze near a bird, it flies away. Not these birds. I shouted. I waved my arms. They all went very quiet. Then – as if to say, *Is that all you've got?* – they walked towards us, silently swinging their carving-knife beaks.

We sprinted for the trees. Ryland tripped on a root. He squirmed around on the ground, waving his arms, shouting, 'Don't leave me!' I helped him back to his feet. He hadn't wanted me to leave him, but he had no problem leaving me. He was gone in an instant. Sprinting towards something that was glinting through the trees. It was a window. A caravan! I ran after him. He dived inside and shut the door in my face.

Considering I had saved Ryland's life at least twice since we got here – three times if you count saving him from starvation with my sandwiches – shutting the door in my face did not show gratitude. I barged in after him while he sat on the floor screaming at me to, 'Shut the door! Don't let them in!'

Ryland more or less filled the caravan by himself. I tried to get him to calm down, but he got up and put all his weight against the back of the door, which nearly made the caravan tip over.

'We are under siege,' he said, 'from birds. They're attacking the door!'

'It's just creaking because you're leaning on it,' I said.

There was a little kitchen and in the kitchen was a cupboard and in the cupboard there was . . . 'Yes! Food!'

'If we are under siege,' I said, 'we'll be sound enough here for a while. Look at all this food.'

'This,' said Ryland, looking along the shelves, 'must be the food bank. In *DogFight Rock*, a ration pick-up like this would seriously enhance your life expectancy.'

I know we don't mention going to the food bank, so I didn't. Even though Ryland mentioned it first. But it was a *bit* like the food bank – the shelves were full of tins: baked beans, tomato soup, a four-pack of Super Noodles, and one and a half jars of peanut butter. Also a jar of Marmite.

'I don't think it's an actual food bank,' I said, 'because the island is uninhabited. But we could use it like a food bank.'

There was a shiny work surface. I lifted it up, and nested away underneath it was a tiny gas hob, some pans and a box of matches. So we had gas, matches, Super Noodles and – remembering the stream we sloshed through earlier – water.

'Ryland,' I said, 'we are on our way to breakfast.'

I asked Ryland to let me out, but he wouldn't move away from the door.

'You can't leave me here with the birds!'

'We need water. Do you want to go and fetch it or shall I?!'

'I'm not going out there.'

The birds had completely lost interest in us the minute we lost interest in their eggs. I ran down the hill to the stream and filled the pot. There were clumps of little white flowers growing along the bank of the stream – they looked and smelt the same as the white flowers that Granny chopped into her magic pasta sauce that day. I put some in my pocket.

Now the mist was gone, I could see the scratchy bush had blackberries on it. I thought, they'll do for a crumble. Going back up the hill with the pan of water, there seemed to be food everywhere. Rabbits kept popping out of the bushes and running away. (Rabbits are edible, aren't they?) Plus obviously the sea is full of fish.

It's true that the rabbits can run fast, and the eggs are protected by evil birds, and getting a fish out of the sea, covering it in batter and putting it on a plate was not exactly a ready meal, but with the sun shining down on all this edible stuff, it made me feel like the whole island was some kind of wild food bank. Nature's Wonder Warehouse.

Back at the caravan, we had a little look around while we were waiting for the water to boil. To be fair, the caravan was mostly bed. A map of the island the size of a tablecloth was spread out on the bed with a pair of binoculars sitting on top of it.

AranOr is much bigger than you'd think. Its coastline squirms around the page like a long piece of spaghetti. I realized I'd definitely need the map to help me find the reset button, so I folded it into my blazer pocket.

Ryland got very excited about the binoculars. 'Have a go,' he said. 'It's like you can touch the jetty! Hey! This could be our headquarters. In *DogFight Rock*, you split into small tribes, find weapons and compete for scarce resources. You and me could be a tribe, and all this food could be the scarce resources – and we've got them all. And also we could keep watch on our enemies with these binoculars.'

I pointed out that this would mean we had all the baked bean and tinned soup resources. But they've got all the jetty resources. 'So they wouldn't get any baked beans. But we wouldn't get, you know, rescued.'

I know Ryland plays *DogFight Rock* a lot, but maybe he doesn't win a lot.

Ryland dropped the binoculars on the bed saying why did people even have binoculars if they weren't going to use them for tribal conflict? I said maybe birdwatching. Ryland could not understand why anyone would want to watch birds. Or have anything to do with birds, unless they were deep fried in a bucket.

'They probably got her,' he said. 'The birdwatcher. All her stuff is here, but she's not here. She's been eaten by the birds.'

I thought it unlikely, but I wasn't going to argue with Ryland over woman-eating birds.

I'd seen something in the caravan that made me stop and think. A couple of hooks on the wall. One had some waterproofs hanging off it. The other had an Aston Villa key ring with one copper key and a silver one, just like the set of keys down at the cottage.

Ryland didn't notice any of that. He was more interested in a phone number written on the bottom of a piece of paper that was Blu-Tacked to the cupboard door. The piece of paper was a timetable of the high and low tide. On the bottom was written: *Spiky Jack* and *Banshee*. I'd heard the word *banshee* before, and not in a good way.

Ryland was saying someone must be in charge of this island, and maybe this was their number. He'd already dialled it before remembering he'd forgotten that his phone didn't work. By then he'd noticed the smell of the cooking.

In case you're interested, I made the most out of the little we had. I simmered the noodles and put a bit of peanut butter on a saucer and let it warm over the pan. When the noodles were cooked, I drained them and threw the warmed peanut butter in straight away, while the noodles were still hot, stirring it round, so it more or less melted into a kind of sauce. Then I slammed the lid on and we legged it down to the jetty before it got cold.

Don't worry, I left a note on the table saying we'd taken some of their tins of beans and some noodles, and peanut butter, oh and the waterproofs, to help us survive on the uninhabited island. I also pointed out that it wasn't uninhabited any more and signed it, *With thanks, Noah Moriarty*.

When we got back, Ryland hammered on the door of the cottages shouting, 'Look what we got!'

Lola was first out. 'You found Mr Merriman!'

'Better than that,' said Ryland.

I'm not sure breakfast would have been better than finding a grown-up who could have rescued us. It is definitely true that saying of Granny's though: '*A big breakfast makes all your troubles look small.*' My whole flock of worries – such as fixing the internet and saving the World – flew away the minute the lid came off the pan and the smell of the noodles steamed out.

Eating it was fun. We didn't have any plates and only two forks, so we had to pass the pan around.

Ada said she couldn't eat it. She said it made her sad to look at it, and what even was it? Then she asked if there were any options.

Ryland said, 'It's Breakfast and the option is No Breakfast.'

'It's kind of like Thai green curry,' said Dario, 'but not green. And without the curry.'

'We could call it Neither Green Nor Curry,' said Ada.

Ryland said he would decide what to call it. He decided to call it Breakfast.

From,

Noah

PS They've picked a leader and it's me. Yes. And I thought breakfast was unexpected. I think waking up and finding we were still all bus-wrecked and eating Super Noodles for breakfast made people realize we might be here for a while. Anyways, it led to an election and, well, I'll tell you about it once I've sorted out the dishes.

MORE SATURDAY

LUNCH MENU

Cowboy Beans & Gold-Digger Mash

Letter 1

To: Mum and Dad
35 Glenarm Terrace, Limavady

Mum and Dad,

You probably think Eve is in charge here because she is a bit bossy at home, but actually it's Lola.

Straight after breakfast, Lola was telling everyone what to do. The fire had gone out and she said we mustn't let that happen again. It was our signal. She said we'd have a rota for watching the fire, and another one for keeping a lookout. She said I was obviously good at food, so I should be in charge of catering. And then she said everyone had to clean their teeth.

When we reminded her that we didn't have toothbrushes, she said it didn't matter. She'd seen an Influencer on YouTube whitening her teeth with ash from a wood fire.

I said, 'Oh! Yes. Our gran said that's what people did when she was little.'

If you think that might make Eve admit publicly that we had the same gran, it didn't. But it did make everyone have a go of cleaning their teeth with ash. It doesn't taste good, but it definitely does the job. We'll have shocking bright smiles when we get rescued.

On the subject of being rescued, Dario said he'd had a good idea. He'd remembered a song about a message in a bottle, so he'd gone to the end of the jetty and thrown his St Anthony of Padua official drinking-water bottle right out into the sea. 'It's probably on the mainland already.'

Eve said, 'What message did you send? In the bottle?'

Dario's face set like jelly. 'I . . . remembered the bottle part of the song,' he said, 'but not the message part.' Then the jelly started to wobble.

Eve said, 'Don't worry. The bottle's got the school badge on it. The motto, even. And by now the police and everyone will be wondering where we are. So the bottle will be a clue. A great clue. And if you'd put a message in it, that'd probably only add to the paperwork. Do you remember what the school motto is, by the way? It's *I was lost, but now I'm found.* So if anyone did find the bottle they'd think, *Oh, That's grand. Nothing for us to do here then.*'

So that's what Eve does. She doesn't boss people, but she asks the right questions and then always tells you the answer. She sort of takes charge without saying so.

'The point is,' said Lola, 'we have to use our initiative and be a credit to the school and stay friends and help each other until someone comes to rescue us. We can do this!'

'No we can't,' said Ryland. 'No one can. People who get stuck on uninhabited islands fight. It always happens. And when there's a fight, some win, some lose . . . and some,' he added, 'get eaten.'

'Well, let's all begin by promising not to eat each other,' said Lola.

That seemed fair enough. Everyone agreed not to eat each other, but getting people to agree to one rule seemed to give Lola an idea for more.

'There's nowhere to charge our phones,' she said, 'so eventually they are going to die, and then even if we do get a signal, we won't be able to use them. So let's have a phone rota. Everyone turns their phones off except one person. Then if the signal comes back, we'll know. And we should put all the phones in one place to be sure that no one is cheating and so we don't lose them, because if you lose a phone when it's switched off, you never find it again. So everyone give your phones to me.'

This made sense to me. But not to Ryland. He was like, 'No one is taking my Switch off me and who said you could tell us what to do?'

'Well, I am the trip First-Aid Officer.' Lola held up the first-aid bag she was wearing around her neck for all of us to see in case we hadn't noticed it.

'The trip is over. It was over when the bus exploded. So –' Ryland folded his arms – 'you can't tell us what to do.'

'We need rules to stop us fighting,' said Lola.

'But we ARE fighting. Your rules are making us fight. You're trying to take my Switch off me, which is stealing, and stealing is not in the rules.'

The situation was getting spicy.

Ada tried to calm things down. 'If anyone is going to be in charge, I was just thinking – since it's his island – it could be the magic child . . .'

Ryland more or less howled. 'Him? Him?!' He pointed at me '*He's* jinxed. Definitely, definitely jinxed. Think about it. Since we met him, everything's gone wrong. Our bus fell off a cliff, we're stuck on an uninhabited island. EVERYTHING NOT SAVED WAS LOST. We should do what they did back in the day and throw The Jinx in the sea. We should let the sharks eat him, like they ate Henry VIII.'

'The fact is,' said Dario, 'sharks did not eat Henry VIII.'

'OK. Who did eat him then?'

'No one ate him! He . . .' Dario looked down at his phone, but it was still blank. 'I don't know,' he said quietly. 'I don't know how Henry VIII died.' He kept staring at the sand as though answers might pop up out of it. 'I don't know how Henry VIII died. I don't know what those birds are called. I didn't know you were supposed to put a message in the bottle. I won't know anything until the phones work again!'

Ryland said, 'Well, I know people are not allowed to steal other people's phones and Switches. Put your hands up if you think—'

But he never got the chance to finish. Because just then, one of the dive-bomber birds plonked itself on the sand, settled its wings behind its back and waddled up to the pan of Neither Green Nor Curry and banged its carving-knife beak against it. The pan rang like a bell, but the bird was not interested in the curry. It looked us all up and down. It seemed to decide that the tastiest doughnut in the drive-through was Ryland. It strolled up and parked itself right in front of him.

'W-what does it want?!' Ryland stammered.

Dario pointed out that none of us spoke Bird.

'I thought Jinx Boy was supposed to be magic,' Ryland snarled, jabbing a finger towards me.

The bird did not like that gesture. It stretched its head right back so that terrible beak was pointing at Ryland's throat. Ryland stepped back, which was a mistake because the bird stabbed its beak into the pocket of his blazer. Ryland was shouting, 'Get it off me!' But just as Ryland didn't speak Bird, so the bird didn't seem to speak Human. It whipped an entire unopened packet of Wee Gems out of Ryland's coat pocket.

Everyone
was pretty
surprised to find
that Ryland had been keeping a MASSIVE sharing
bag of sweets to himself.

'They're mine!'

The bird did not care. It slapped the packet of Wee
Gems on a rock then chopped at it with its beak until
the sweets fell out. It took one sweet, hoisted up its
head and swallowed it. Then it did it again. And again.

Ryland was jabbering by now. 'See! I told you. He's
trained one of his devil birds to attack me.'

'The birds –' Ada sighed – 'obey him. Even the bad
birds.'

'Gannet!' Dario whooped. 'I've just remembered.
That bird is a gannet. I've remembered something.'

The gannet looked up as though it recognized its name. It also seemed to decide it didn't like jelly sweets. It wandered off.

'I do like Wee Gems,' said Ada. 'Would anyone mind if I—'

'They're mine,' said Ryland.

'I'm not sure how hygienic that is anyway,' said Eve.

Ada had to admit that the bird had touched the Wee Gems, but, she pointed out, it did seem like it kept itself very clean, for a bird. 'Look how white his wings are. Like an angel. And he's got kind of eyeliner on, which I like.'

Ada was right. The gannet does have these black feathers around its eyes, which do look good.

'Why is everyone being nice about his bird?' said Ryland. 'The bird mugged me off for my sugar rush. That bird is rogue.' He tried to shove it away with his foot, but turns out that gannets can take rejection. This one snuggled up to Ryland's leg.

It was funny, but Lola said it was wrong to laugh at others. Then her phone beeped an alert. 'That means morning assembly.'

Ryland said that one good thing about being bus-wrecked was at least we didn't have to do assembly.

Dario pointed out that it was Saturday, so there was no assembly.

'We are on a school trip,' said Lola, 'so this is a school day. I've told my phone they're all school days until further notice. We need to stick to the timetable.' Then she basically did the whole assembly right there, off the top of her head. It was all about how she believed in us, and we should all believe in each other. She finished with a prayer to St Anthony of Padua, patron saint of our school, and famous for helping people find lost things. For instance, us. She asked him to help us find Mr Merriman, and she said our mums and dads were definitely praying that they would find their lost children, so please would St Anthony answer their prayers. Then she said, 'Right. We've had breakfast, brushed our teeth, had assembly – let's get going.'

No one moved.

Get going doing what? It was the gannet who answered that question. Well the gannet and our Eve.

While Lola was still talking, the gannet slid over to me, whipped the map out of my pocket and dropped it on the sand. Eve picked it up.

'He stole that,' said Ryland. 'From the caravan. Why are you going round stealing maps?'

I remembered what you said, Dad, in your letter about not telling anyone. So I did not say, *I've borrowed it to help me find the island's internet box because I've broken the internet.* Instead I said, 'This is an ancient treasure map. There's a golden treasure buried here on the island of AranOr. If you help me find it, I'll share it with you.'

I don't know where that idea came from. I think it was because I'd noticed a little 'X' in the middle of the map, and 'X marks the spot' is what they always say about treasure maps. Anyway, I was absolutely sure that Eve would think I'd gone too far now.

Eve was looking at the map really hard. I was sure she was going to say, *Take no notice. This is my unusually little, little brother, who has illegally bunked into our school trip.* But she didn't say any of that. She said, 'Amazing. This really is a treasure map.'

She held it up for the others to see. It had the words 'TREASURE MAP' written in big blue letters across the top. I'd never noticed that before. 'This Wee Gem,' Eve said, pointing at me, 'really is going to lead us to buried treasure.'

From,

Noah

TO: The Wee Gem
Sea View Cottage, AranOr

Dear Wee Gem,
Eve knows there's no treasure on the island, really.

But she also knows that, now and then, everyone needs a wee bit of make-believe. To help with the difficult things in life. Think about when we first started with the food bank, and Mum used to tell you we had won free food so you wouldn't know we had money trouble.

So buried treasure is a great front for finding the internet box. If the others think they're looking for treasure, they'll be happy.

Nice work, there.

Think about what you're looking for. That reset button is one of the most important things in the World. It connects two halves of the planet. It's not going to be sitting there in a wee metal box on a beach. It's going to be in the safest, most weather-proof and earthquake-proof building on the island.

Maybe that's what the X means on your map?

Like you said, Eve knows the right questions and then she answers them.

The question right now is - what does the X mean on that map?

Get on with it.

Dad

Letter 2

To: Mum and Dad Moriarty
35 Glenarm Terrace, Limavady

Dear Mum and Dad and Everyone,

You'd think if you suddenly announced that you'd found a treasure map, no one would believe you. But no. Everyone believed me. It was as if buried treasure was only to be expected.

Dario said that historically there was nearly bound to be treasure here because of the Spanish Armada. 'The Spanish Armada got blown off course around Ireland. Fun fact. Most of those ships weren't for fighting. They were carrying food and gold to pay the soldiers. They were absolutely wedged with gold.'

To hear him talk, doubloons and moidore and pieces of eight were probably being washed up on our beach by every tide.

Ada said that an island like this one – which wasn't even on a human-made map – was exactly the kind of place where the faeries and leprechauns would hide their gold.

I wanted to say, *What are you talking about!? This*

island actually IS on a human-made map. This map!
The one you are literally holding in your hand right now!
Somehow I stopped myself.

Ryland thought the presence of treasure explained the absence of Mr Merriman. 'He probably knew about it all along and brought us here to help him find it. But probably rival treasure hunters found out and killed him. We are probably next on the list, so I think we should go home.'

'The point is,' said Lola. 'This is our chance to shine. Team St Anthony's is going to find buried treasure. Go, Team Tony Padua! Go Wee Gem!'

It turned out we couldn't just 'go', because no one seemed to know how a map worked.

Ryland looked hard at it and said, 'Where even are we on this map?'

Eve pointed to the jetty and said, 'That's the jetty, so these little squares are Sea View Cottage, that's the shop, and this here is our beach.'

'But where are WE? There should be a little blue dot.'

Eve explained that the blue dot only moved around on phones and computers, not on paper maps.

'So where are we then?' said Lola.

I realized she thought there should be a little YOU ARE HERE symbol somewhere on the map.

'You're not actually marked on the map, because the map was made before you came here,' I said, 'probably long ago. In the Armada times.'

It was scary how good I was at lying to them.

'Or maybe in the time of the great war between the faeries and the humans,' said Ada.

Eve decided to move things on.

'The really interesting question,' she said, 'isn't where WE are. It's where the treasure is. There should be clues.'

Clues. I hadn't thought about clues. How was I going to give them clues when there wasn't any treasure to give them clues to? It was because I was thinking about this that I didn't notice at first that the others were all jumping up and down and pointing at something in the sky.

'Is it a bird?' asked Ryland. 'Another horrible bird.'

'Is it a plane?' called Dario.

'Is it a faerie?' said Ada.

But it wasn't a bird.

We could hear an engine buzzing now and see that it wasn't flapping, but wobbling through the air towards us.

'A helicopter! A rescue helicopter!' whooped Lola.

'Yes!' cheered Ryland.

'They probably found your message in a bottle,' said Lola. 'Or at least the bottle with no message. Is it me, by the way, or does that helicopter look surprisingly small?'

'It looks small because it's far away,' said Dario. 'It's called perspective. It will get bigger as it gets nearer . . .'

But it was already pretty near and it was still pretty small. In fact it was right over our heads. It was not a helicopter. It looked exactly like a pair of low-flying frying pans with propellers, with a huge package dangling from it.

'It's a delivery drone,' said Eve. 'Where's it going?'

A delivery!

We chased after it.

We were probably all wondering what was inside – an inflatable rescue boat? A tent? Tons of food?

I was feeling relieved. Someone was sending us a package – that meant maybe I was wrong. Maybe someone did know where we were. Someone kind enough to send a us an aid package. Someone who would definitely come and rescue us.

The drone hovered just above the roof of Sea View Cottage and released its package. The box clattered through the hole in the broken thatch and thumped on to the rickety old table, shattering it into matchwood. A great hank of wet thatch flopped on to the box, splitting it down the middle.

'Rude,' said Lola. 'And after all the tidying up we did.'

Every one of us was probably expecting to find something different inside. But it's a good bet that no one was expecting to find a shocking-pink, self-locking, waterproof 250-litre roof box.

'What even is it?' said Ryland.

'The fact is,' Dario explained, 'that's a shocking-pink, waterproof roof box for storing and transporting luggage on the roof of your car.'

'But we haven't got a car,' said Ryland.

'How very true,' said Dario. 'Ours fell off a cliff.'

*

They were all so sad and disappointed about the parcel that I could see they'd forgotten about the treasure hunt. That's honestly the only reason I said, 'A clue!'

Everyone stared at me. I stared at Eve, daring her finally to say something.

'You asked for a clue,' I said. 'This is it.'

And then Eve finally did say something.

She'd been rummaging through the packaging inside the box. Now she stood up, holding a piece of paper that looked a lot like the receipt.

'This,' she said, 'is the first clue . . .' She read out a little rhyme. '*Under the ground, it cannot shine – your treasure lies sleeping in a straight line.*'

'How –' Ada gulped, pointing at me – 'did he do that? How did Magic Child make a clue appear out of the sky like that?'

'And why,' said Ryland, pointing to the pink roof box, 'would you put two little sentences in a massive plastic box.'

'In case,' I said, 'it fell in the sea. Obviously.'

Everyone seemed to agree that a 250-litre plastic box was obviously the best way to deliver a poem. No one seemed to think that it might have come to the wrong address. When we tidied the box and the packaging out of our now not-so-nice-and-clean cottage, I made sure I was the one tidying all the paperwork.

I found the real address on it.

The box came from the actual Orinoco Wonder Warehouse, Letterkenny. It was strange, looking at that box, thinking that maybe just a wee while ago it was in the place where we were supposed to be. And now it was stranded just like us. It was addressed to somewhere in Germany. It must have been trying to get there the long way round – across the Atlantic and the Pacific oceans. I didn't say it out loud, but I couldn't help but wonder if this was another clue that something was going very wrong in the rest of the World.

It made me worry about what was happening to you all at home.

It made me want to find the internet box and fix things as quick as I could.

I looked up from the tidying up and there was no sign of the others. Which was just as well because I had to get rid of the paper with the address on, in case the others saw it and started asking questions. The only thing I could think of doing with it was chuck it in the fire.

Eve was already sitting down outside with the map spread out on the sand and the others surrounding her.

'In the clue,' she was saying, 'it says the treasure is in a straight line. So if we draw a straight line from here . . .' She used a strip of cardboard from the packaging and drew a straight line from the jetty right across the island. It went up over the hill and down to what looked like another beach. 'All we have to do,' she said, 'is follow that line and keep our eyes open for anything unusual.'

The cabinet I stood on is by the jetty, and the cable must go on from there in a straight line across the island. Somewhere on that straight line I might find the internet box or a sign, or something I can press or pull to restart the internet.

All we had to do was follow that line. It was almost as if Eve knew all this. I tried to catch her eye, but she didn't look at me. She did exactly what you'd do if you wanted little kids to do something.

'Lola,' she said, 'can we walk in a straight line, d'you think?'

'We are the mighty St Anthony's,' said Lola, 'We can do this! Yay!'

So off we went.

I'll write and tell you what happened when I've got time. Unless you've come and rescued us before then. Then I could tell you face to face, which would be the best.

From,

Noah

Letter 3

To: Dad
35 Glenarm Terrace, Limavady

Dear Dad,

Walking in a straight line is harder than you think.

The line on the map went past cottages, and the phone box, and the letter box. A few minutes later, we were at the stream.

'I didn't know there was a river,' said Dario, as we sloshed through it.

I mentioned that this was where I'd got the water for the Breakfast. This outraged Ryland.

'You didn't tell me that you picked water up off the ground. The muddy ground! I thought you got it from the tap, not from a river. You can't just drink a river!'

'We didn't drink the whole river,' I said. 'Just a couple of panfuls.'

To be honest, we didn't even drink it. We just cooked in it.

Maybe it was because we were talking, but soon after that, Eve realized the line we'd been walking had somehow got wiggly.

'Look at the map,' she said. 'The line passes through

the edge of the woods, but there are no woods here.'

To be fair, there were no woods to be seen. Except the tops of a few trees sticking over the crest of a hill to the right.

'The woods have moved!' cried Ada. 'The spirits of the trees don't want us to find the treasure.'

'Is one possible explanation,' agreed Eve.

'Or the map is out of date,' said Dario. 'And the trees have all been chopped down.'

'Again, possible.'

'Those little pointy things on the map,' said Ryland. 'Are they definitely supposed to be trees? They look more like umbrellas.'

'Maybe,' said Eve. 'Though it's hard to see why there would be a field full of umbrellas in the middle of an island.'

'Where is this line, anyway?' said Ryland, looking up and down the hill. 'I can't see it.'

'The line is on the map,' explained Eve. 'There's no line on the ground.'

'Well no wonder we can't see it then.'

Eve said she thought we may have got slightly lost and we should go back to the beginning. 'Lola, can we retrace our steps?'

'Yes, we can!' whooped Lola. 'Come on, Team St Anthony – let's retrace!'

So we went back to the beginning and started again.

The sun was getting higher. We were getting sticky and thirsty.

'Don't worry,' said Lola. 'I used to be in the majorettes.'

At first I couldn't see why that helped. Being a majorette involves marching up and down while throwing a twinkly stick in the air in time to some music.

It turns out that walking in straight lines is the most important part of being a majorette. And Lola was a genius at walking in a straight line.

She did it like this. She made us all stand at the jetty. Then she walked to the phone box and shouted back at us, 'This is our line. To continue it, we need one person – that's you, Dario – to walk past me, then stop when I say so . . .' Dario did that. 'Now,' she yelled, 'Dario look back and make sure that me, you and Eve are in a straight line.' He squinted back at us all, then gave a thumbs-up. Then Lola made Ada walk on past Dario, and then she had to look back. This went on till we were all in a line, and Lola was at the back. Then she left the phone box and walked past us all before looking back. It was a relay.

Walking in a straight line is hard work, and you probably need at least one majorette to help you. I'd say the ideal would be to find a majorette who didn't keep shouting that you should swing your arms and smile when walking, and didn't insist that everyone cheer every time the line was straight.

Lola is not that person.

Although we walked for miles in a straight line, there was no sign of the kind of building that might have an internet box inside. Or any other kind of building. Or treasure.

I realized that if I didn't find it today, I'd need to remember where we'd already looked. To do that, we'd need to write all the places we'd been on to the map.

Back home we had door numbers and names of streets and roads and buildings and signposts and coffee shops and pubs with names to help us find our way.

On AranOr, we had to imagine an invisible road and find our own landmarks. We had to start noticing things geographically. It wasn't easy because we didn't know the names of the trees or the bushes or the rocks. So we made up new names for them.

For instance, Ryland was standing by a big bush whose pretty little yellow flowers did not make up for the nasty sharpness of its long black thorns. We called it Furious Yellow.

The big rock with the dive-bomber birds was christened Gannet Rock, now that Dario had remembered what the birds were called.

There was a round thing in one of the trees that looked a bit like a cardboard football with an eye-shaped hole in the bottom. We called it Cardboard CCTV, until we realized it was a wasp nest full of wasps. After that we called it a Wasp Nest.

If there was nothing interesting where we were standing, then we put something interesting there. For instance, just over the crest of the hill, where you could easily miss the straight line, there was a pile of stones.

Eve was about to write this down on the map as 'Pile of Stones' when Dario pointed out that there might be other piles of stones. 'People have been making piles of stones since the Stone Age,' he said. 'You need to give this one a name.'

Lola wanted to name it the St Anthony High's High Pile of Stones.

Eve pointed out that was not actually true, because they weren't our stones and we didn't make them into a pile.

Ada agreed. She was concerned that if some faeries had made the pile, they might get angry with us for trying to take the credit. She mentioned some of the things that faeries do when they are angry.

Although the rest of us did not believe in faeries, we did all agree that it was not worth the risk. Ada suggested that we call it the Pooka Pile because the Pooka is some kind of furry faerie who lives in stones.

We stuck with that because it sounded good.

It was only when I went to mark it on the map that I realized that the Pooka Pile was nearly exactly where the X was. I know you said that the box would be inside the safest, most weather-and-earthquake-proof building on the island. But that can't be a four-foot-high pile of Stone Age stones, can it?

Ryland was looking at the map over my shoulder. 'X marks the spot,' he said. 'Isn't the treasure supposed to be here? Is this the treasure? A bunch of old rocks?'

He picked up one of the stones and threw it.

Ada was horrified. 'If we get any trouble from the Pooka,' she said, 'that's on you.'

Dario pointed out that treasure is usually buried. But no one had a spade, and everyone was getting hot and sweaty, so we sat down on top of a broken wall covered in bright yellow moss.

Ada wanted to call this the Couch of Gold because the moss looked comfy yet gold. But when we sat on the mossy cushion, it tipped us all backwards. Which is when we discovered the wall was actually part of a gravestone.

We all pretended to be scared of the grave and ran away, laughing.

The straight line led us to treasure in the end. Just not the treasure we'd been looking for.

We'd reached a burn. It was deep, and the water was bright and clear except where it ran over some rocks, when it gave itself little crowns of white bubbles. It rushed on down a steep hill and through a narrow gap between two big white boulders.

We heard it ages before we saw it.

I actually thought it was the sound of traffic.

Ada thought it was faerie laughter.

Eve strode through the gap, with Lola trying to pull her back, saying, 'What if it's something really bad?'

It was a waterfall.

Just a few feet beyond us, the burn chucked itself off the rocks and down into a deep, dark gully with a pool at the bottom where the falling water churned and rolled like when you're boiling pasta. Except it looked really cold, and it shone as it roared.

We all really wanted to jump in.

'We can't though, can we?' said Ryland. 'Not without permission?'

Permission was the last thing Ryland usually worried about.

'Whose permission?' said Lola. 'There's no grown-ups around.'

Lola looked at me. I couldn't figure out why, until she said, 'I suppose it's up to the Wee Gem.'

Until then I had never really understood that being the leader could be a problem. I mean what if I said,

Yes, OK, all jump in – and then they were dashed to smithereens on the rocks? Their fates would be all on me.

I looked at our Eve, wishing she would finally help me out. She just turned away from me and said, 'Look!'

She was pointing to a narrow ledge that snaked behind the waterfall.

'We could walk behind a waterfall! Without getting wet.'

So we did. We all shuffled along this shiny wet ledge with sheets of water roaring past our noses. Ada, in fact, leaned forward and let her nose touch the water. 'Oh!' she shrieked. 'It's so wet.'

'That's because,' said Dario, 'it's water.'

'I suppose,' Ada said.

Then – just to check – she pushed her head through the fall, letting the water drape itself over her shoulders, like a towel.

'Yes,' she said. 'It's wet. And it's cold!' She shuddered. 'It's really, really cold. I'm so cold I can't even feel the cold.'

Ryland carefully pushed his hand into the curtain of water.

'That,' he said, 'is force. That's so force. It nearly knocked me over.' He turned to face me. 'So is the Wee Gem going to jump, or what?'

My answer was drowned out by a scream. Then

by a lot more screams bouncing off the rocks. Then a splash. Ada had slipped off the edge.

For ages we didn't hear anything but the sound of water. And the sound of Ryland saying, 'She's dead. She's dead,' over and over. Then we heard a whoop and a holler and a shout of, 'Come down! This is wondrous!' So we knew that she wasn't dead.

'Who's next?' said Dario.

'Are you saying I'm scared?' growled Ryland.

'No, I'm saying who's next? Are you next?'

'No,' said Lola. 'He's not because . . .'

She was the next to jump through the waterfall and into the pool.

Dario went after her.

Down below, the others cheered as he splashed down. Then it was just me and Eve and Ryland.

Eve offered Ryland the map, saying someone needed to look after it and keep it dry.

He said, 'You mean you're going to jump? And leave me up here, and everyone's going to say I was the only one who didn't jump?!'

'Someone really does need to look after this map . . .'

Ryland pushed his Switch into my arms, said, 'Look after this,' and jumped.

So then it was just me and Eve.

It was the first time there was just the two of us since we were bus-wrecked. I had loads of things to tell

her. I tried. I pulled out the letter. I said,
'Look at this. It's from Dad.'

Did she try to grab it out of my
hand and devour its words with a
homesick heart? No. She shoved the
map at me, said, 'Look after this,' and
jumped through the waterfall.

So then it was just me and the map
at the top of the waterfall.

Looking down, I could see a little
rainbow hovering over the water.
It seemed to dance in time to the
laughter and the splashing that was
flying up from the pool. Ada was
probably already planning to call it the
Faerie Falls or the Laughing Waters or
something magical. But I wrote 'Our
Waterfall' on the map because, just
then, that's how it felt.

We'd been calling AranOr an
uninhabited island, but it wasn't

uninhabited at all. We were the inhabitants. Just us.

I sat on the ledge thinking, *How class is this?!*

We've got our own island.

There's no one here but us.

In the middle of the sea, a kingdom of kids.

Well, kids and Mr Merriman – wherever he was.

Then I noticed another sound. Not laughter or rushing water or birds calling.

It was really faint and far away.

I got up to the top, away from the rumble of the waterfall.

Bells! Tiny bells were ringing.

I knew that sound from somewhere.

Then I recognized it. It was the sound of an old-fashioned phone ringing! That's how quiet the island was. You could hear a phone ring half a mile away

I bounced down that path.

I sloshed through that stream.

I killed the whole run from Our Waterfall right down to the phone box.

The others were bashing through the bushes behind me. They'd heard it too. It was a race, and I won it.

I grabbed the door handle. And the moment I put my hand on the door, the phone stopped ringing.

Eve squelched past me. She grabbed the phone. It gave a little last jingle. But it had rung itself to sleep.

No one said a word. We all just stood there in a

circle, staring at the silent phone. The only sound was the water dripping from our clothes and hair.

Without saying anything, we all knew we were waiting to see if it would ring again. And trying to imagine who it was that had rung. Maybe Mr Merriman? Or school? Or the coastguard? Maybe someone who used to live in Sea View Cottage, someone who hadn't heard that they'd all moved away.

The phone didn't ring again.

Someone's stomach rumbled.

Lola shivered and said she was cold.

When you're cold and wet, there should be someone there waiting for you, with a bag of hot chips or a pan of warm stew.

At home it would be you or Mum.

Here on AranOr it was me.

Ada was good at names.

Lola was good at straight lines.

I am good at food. Just like you said, Dad.

So I grabbed Eve's backpack and slipped away.

Got to go.

Don't worry about me. But do come and rescue us if you can.

From,

Noah

Letter 4

To: The Moriarty Family
35 Glenarm Terrace, Limavady

Dear Mum, Dad, Baby Isabella (and Granny Nuala also),

I was trying to make everything normal, but rogue things keep happening.

The most rogue one was in the middle of the night. But I'll tell you about that later. First I need to tell you about the caravan.

I'd remembered all the tins of food, and was planning on stuffing them into Eve's rucksack for a surprise feast. But when I got to it, the caravan door, which I definitely closed behind me earlier, was open.

Someone had opened it. Maybe they were still in there?

I shouted, 'Hello?'

No answer.

It was just starting to rain – that soft rain you can hardly feel. If someone was in there, they'd definitely shut the door to keep the rain out.

I stuck my head around the door.

The place was empty.

There were no papers on the table. No books on the floor. No litter in the bin. No keys on the hook. Someone had been and cleaned the place out. They'd even taken the gas hob.

I called, 'Hello?' again.

No answer.

I stepped inside.

The shelves were still full. Which was mysterious. I mean if you're stuck on an uninhabited island, what could be more precious and exciting than tins of baked beans, not to mention sweetcorn, tuna and tomatoes? I mean you've got the makings of a decent dinner right there.

I stuffed the tinned tomatoes into the backpack. Held my breath. What if whoever had turned the place over was hiding somewhere? What if they jumped out and said, *Who's that stealing my tinned goods?!* and whacked me over the head with one of the frying pans? No one did.

I took the tuna. Still no scary tin-owner. I went for baked beans, sweetcorn, and the box of matches sitting next to the stove.

I shouted, 'Thanks! We'll pay you back when we get rescued!' Then I ran.

The tins in the backpack jangled and dinged like an unanswered phone, which is what everyone thought it was when I ran on to the beach.

They all sat up and gave me the kind of look you might give Santa if he burst into your bedroom on Christmas Eve carrying a big sack. Then they realized it wasn't a phone ringing, and gave me the kind of look you might give if Santa said Christmas was cancelled.

They were disappointed, but I was confident of undisappointing them.

'I have brought you,' I said, 'a feast.'

I tipped the backpack upside down so the tins rolled out, flashing in the sunlight.

'Tins,' said Dario. 'Great. So –' he looked around the place – 'who's got a tin opener?'

Nowadays most tins come with a ring pull, so you just peel the lid off. Whoever had put the tins in the caravan was against that. These were all old-fashioned tins – the kind that looks at you as if to say, *Yes there's food inside me, but if you want it, you'll have to fight me for it.*

I suppose I could have volunteered to go back to the caravan and look for a tin opener, but if I did that Ryland might come with me and find out our HQ had been raided and panic.

And to be fair, I was so creeped out that I had already decided I was never going to go back to that caravan again. Even if there was a tin opener in there.

'If it's any use,' said Ada, 'I have a knife.'

If she'd said, *I can breathe fire, by the way*, that would have been less surprising and more useful.

'What made you bring a knife on a school trip?' asked Lola.

Dario said he wasn't even sure it was legal.

'I just really like the handle,' said Ada.

The knife had a wooden handle covered in tiny carvings of leaves and berries. If a faerie murderer was going to stab you, this would be its weapon of choice. It looked like one nick from its blade would turn you into sunbeams or whatever.

It had very little effect on a tin of beans though. The blade snapped off and went cartwheeling through the air and caught Ryland on the ear.

This led to a lot of shouting and blaming, but it did not lead to baked beans.

Meanwhile, the tin just sat there, its unopened lid shining in the afternoon sun.

Ryland tried hitting it with a big sharp stone. This knocked the tin on to its side and set it rolling down the sand.

Dario said he'd read something on the internet about a good way to open tin cans if you don't have a can opener. But he couldn't remember what it was, and when he tried to pick up the tin, something snatched it out of his fingers.

Ryland's gannet.

It grabbed the tin and spiralled off with it wedged in its beak.

'Ah,' said Dario. 'I remember now. This is what gannets do when they find a big crab or a lobster. They soar as high as they can go and then they . . . OH!'

The rest of the sentence should have been . . . *drop them from a great height so that they smash to bits*. Dario didn't need to say that, because it's exactly what the gannet did with the tin of beans. It just let go and let the tin drop like a hammer from the sky. It hit a rock, then bounced up and hit Ryland.

'I hate this tin!' Ryland wheezed, chucking the tin away. 'I hate this island. I'm going home.'

He grabbed the map off Eve.

'Is that the sea there?' said Ryland, pointing at the blue between the island and the mainland.

Yes it was the sea.

'It says *Sound*.'

'*The Sound of Or*,' read Eve. 'It's the name of this bit of the sea.'

'*Sound* means all right,' said Ryland. 'It says the sea is sound here. And it doesn't look very far. I can walk across three centimetres. I'm going home.'

'I don't think so. . .' Eve tried to explain about scale and maps, but Ryland was already striding towards the water.

'Ryland, it's miles. You'll drown. Or die of cold.'

'It's better than waiting till the Jinx Kid's evil birds kill us all,' he yelled back.

As he said this, the gannet launched itself into the air and flapped out to sea. A few seconds later it was just a white dot against the faraway blue mountain.

'Look at it!' called Ryland. 'It's nearly back on the mainland already. I'm off home.'

There's a lot of big rocks sticking up out of the shallow water of the bay and off into sea. Ryland stepped and jumped from one to the other until he was – got to admit – quite a way from the beach. From where I was standing, it looked like he was walking on the water.

I had to stop him. I was going to tell them the truth.

'Ryland, listen!' I shouted. 'This is the island where the internet cable comes in across the sea from America. Or to America. It goes both ways.'

'What's that got to do with anything?' snarled Ryland. 'Phones don't work off cables. They work off satellites.'

'The fact is,' said Dario, 'the internet does come by cable from America to Ireland. The cable is called . . . I've forgotten again. I used to know. Or I thought I did. Maybe it was my phone that knew everything, not me. Anyway there is definitely a cable. They use cables because cables have more bandwidth than satellites. Oh. And fun fact – sharks are attracted to the cables. They chew them. Apparently it gives them a buzz.'

The bit about sharks made Ryland stop for a second. But only a second.

'You're just trying to scare me,' he snapped. 'I bet I can get across without even getting my feet wet.'

I sort of wish I'd made that bet now, because I would have won.

Ryland's feet did get wet. Also his head, chest and middle. Because when he jumped to the next rock, it wasn't there. He plunged into the cold waters and bellowed for help.

It turns out that Ryland is good at jumping into water but not so good at swimming about in it. He sank.

Everyone ran to help him. Tiptoeing over the tops of the rocks. Only Eve was smart and brave enough to dive straight into the water, swim out, and drag him back to shore.

She didn't need to drag him far because, turns out, the sea was not that deep. All Eve had to do was make Ryland stand up and he was safe. Safe but very, very wet and cold.

They trudged back up the beach, shuddering and spluttering and saying, 'I'm so cold,' over and over.

School uniform does not make the best swimming gear.

Ryland's pockets were like a pair of little buckets full of water. He fished his phone out of one of them with a sob of despair.

'I hear you can dry phones out if you stick them in a packet of rice,' said Lola.

'Quick. Fetch a packet of rice. Oh wait,' Ryland snarled, 'we don't have any rice.'

I remembered I had that box of matches I'd found in the caravan in my pocket.

I lit the bonfire, and we huddled round it, toasting our toes.

We put Ryland's phone on a rock near the fire to dry out, as if it was a wet puppy.

Without anyone else noticing it happening, the gannet turned up again and waddled into the best place by the fire. Its neck was swollen. It looked like something was moving around in there. Then it put its head back and made a disgusting gulping noise.

Dario explained that it was swallowing a fish.

'I was watching it,' he said. 'It flew up really high, then dropped like a stone into the sea. It must've caught a fish and brought it back here to eat. Sociable.'

The bird sat there watching us and munching

its fish, as though it was munching popcorn while watching a movie.

And what kind of movie would we be? Some kind of horror film where we all end up eating each other, like Ryland said? *The Really Hungry Hunger Games*? A movie where everyone could be saved if they got up and helped look for the button that could reset the internet and save the World, but they'd rather sit on the beach, waiting for a ship that was never going to come?

I couldn't let that happen.

Ryland and Eve's uniform was dripping wet.

Ada said that her great granny told her the faeries used those yellow bushes as washing lines, to dry their clothes and gossamer wings.

Eve pointed out that they didn't have anything to change into while they were drying, but I remembered the waterproofs we'd brought down from the caravan, and I ran off to get them.

When I came back, Eve said thank you. I think they were the first words she'd spoken to me since we were bus-wrecked.

Sitting by the fire, watching the steam come off their clothes, the others seemed happy enough, but the tops of the tins glowed with its flames, the food inside taunting me.

Dario must have read my mind.

'Did you know,' said Dario, 'that tin openers weren't invented until a hundred years after tinned food?'

'What,' said Lola, 'are you saying? That people put food in tins and left it for a hundred years without opening them?'

'No. They opened them, but not with tin openers. The first canned food was used by the Dutch Navy in the eighteenth century, but the first tin opener was invented in London by a man who made surgical instruments about a hundred years later. I can't remember his name.'

'We don't care about his name,' said Ryland. 'We care about the food.'

'How did the navy get the food out of the tins if they didn't have tin openers?' said Eve, and for once she didn't seem to know the answer to her own question.

'I think . . .' began Dario. 'No. Sorry. Forgotten that too. I mean they were the navy, so they had harpoons and cannons and stuff.'

Then Ada shouted out, 'Look! The final clue!!!'

The 'clue' was a rainbow, arching up from the trees and coming down somewhere behind Sea View Cottage. Everyone agreed that it was pretty. No one could see how it was a clue.

Ada explained that it was well known that leprechauns were forever hiding gold at the end of rainbows. I thought this did not say a lot for the wisdom of leprechauns. Why would you hide your gold at the end of something that disappears as soon as the sun comes out? If leprechauns are real, they really need someone to tell them about banks.

Dario said, 'You can't get to the end of the rainbow because it's always moving.'

'Let's go and see,' said Eve, with one of her do-as-you're-told/don't-ask-questions looks.

Dario turned out to be wrong about it being impossible to get to the end of a rainbow, because when we scrambled through the cottage and pushed open the back door, there it was, just standing there in the field behind the house.

In case you want to know what the end of a rainbow looks like, this one looked like a blue-and-yellow ghost that had decided to haunt a big fat tractor tyre and some plants.

'The gold!' whooped Ada, pointing at the plants. 'And it's just like the clue said – *in a straight line.*'

The plants had little pink flowers with a bright yellow bit in the middle, and where the rainbow touched them, they really did shine like little gold pieces. And I had to admit, they were indeed in a very straight line.

Ada was sadly disappointed that there wasn't a heap of gold coins sitting there. But that didn't stop her. 'I remember now,' she said. 'The clue said, *Under the ground, it cannot shine.* So the gold must be underneath. Has anyone got a spade?'

This did not sound like a sensible question, but funnily enough, there was a spade leaning against the broken garden wall.

Somehow, it turned out that the best way to find out whether or not Ada was right was for me to dig with all my might while she pointed at things.

I didn't ask, *Why me?* because I knew the answer was, *Because the littlest is the easiest to boss around.*

There was no gold.

When I dug into the ground, the plants turned out to be attached to knobbly brown things.

'Does anyone else think these look familiar?' I said, holding one up.

Eve cut into one with a little kitchen knife she found at the back of a drawer in the cottage.

'Spuds!' I shouted. 'Ada, you found a field full of spuds. That's actually better than gold!'

Whoever used to live here had planted half a field of potatoes, in neat long rows. The potatoes had carried on growing, even though the people had left.

We dug up as many as we could carry. Lola said that she was sure it wasn't safe to eat anything that had been underground, and anyway how did we know they were real potatoes if they didn't have labels on.

*

It was only when we got back to the beach that we realized that Ryland hadn't come up to the cottage. He was rocking backwards and forwards by the fire, with a tin in his hand, rubbing the tin on a stone. He looked like one of those very sad gorillas that you sometimes see in a zoo.

I thought the prospect of spuds might cheer him up, but I got the feeling he wanted to be left alone from the way he shouted, 'Just leave me alone!'

We took turns peeling the spuds – one using the knife from Sea View Cottage, and the other the broken blade of Ada's faerie knife. If the faeries had bestowed any magical powers upon that knife, sadly spud-peeling was not one of them.

Being honest, I was insanely excited about those spuds.

I was thinking about making them into roasties or chips. But the spuds had no ambitions to be chips. They put up more of a fight than the tins did, even. And the knives were not necessarily on our side. The knives didn't mind if they were peeling potatoes or peeling you. And no matter how much skin you thought you'd cut off a potato, there was always a bit more lurking round the corner.

Then when we were starting to lose all hope, Ryland shouted, 'Done it!'

He had got the lid off the tin of beans.

He'd scraped the rim over and over on the rock until it just sort of got worn out and the lid just lifted off. 'Everything's got a weak spot,' he said. 'Even a tin.'

Somehow the next few spuds were easy.

We got a pan of water from the stream, boiled it up, and when they were ready, mixed the potatoes in with the beans and passed the pan around. Dario said this was exactly what cowboys ate when they were on the trail.

Maybe it was because we'd worked so hard to get the ingredients. Maybe it was because the evening star came out just as we started eating. Whatever it was, that was the best meal ever.

After we'd eaten, Lola made sure everyone brushed their teeth and said prayers.

I asked St Anthony of Padua to help someone find us.

'We are lost,' I said, 'and you are in charge of finding lost things. Please help someone find us.'

'But not before you help us find the gold,' said Ryland. And everyone laughed.

'Or the big warehouse,' said Lola. 'We could get little faerie lights or bedside lamps so it didn't have to be quite so dark when the sun went down.'

'Or a kettle, so we could have a decent cup of tea,'

said Dario. 'And milk. I'm missing milk. I never expected to miss milk.'

Ryland said he didn't miss milk, but he did miss red lemonade.

I realized they were all looking at their maps of the Wonder Warehouse again. Yesterday we were talking like we might be rescued any minute. One day later, we were talking like this was normal life now.

But then – and this is the whole point of this letter – remember what I said about rogue stuff happening? Well, something *really* rogue happened.

In the dead of night.

A bell rang.

Not a church bell far away. But that little *ding* an old-fashioned phone makes when you put the receiver down.

Someone was out there. In the phone box.

Even though it was the middle of the night and dead dark, I slipped out of the hammock.

I could just make out a shadow in the moonlight, hunched over the phone.

A voice was muttering. That little bell dinged again. The phantom phoner had hung up.

I ducked behind the wall. The door of the phone box creaked open. A figure shambled out into the moonlight.

I didn't see what happened next because I was back

in the hammock with my school coat pulled over my head as quick as blinking.

Had the caravan-raiding ghost come to haunt the phone box?

That thought stopped me going back to sleep. What if Sea View Cottage was next?

From,

Noah

PS I really want you to come and rescue us, please.

SUNDAY

SUNDAY BRUNCH MENU

Catch of the Day
Garlic-Smoked Teeny Tiny Fish

Letter 1

To: Mr Moriarty
35 Glenarm Terrace, Limavady

Dear Dad,

I'm thinking about all the times you asked me to go fishing with you and I said no. Now I wish I'd said yes.

This is what I know about fishing:

- You put a bait on a hook
- You put the hook in the water
- The fish eats the bait
- The hook catches the fish
- You eat the fish

It turns out this is just a theory.

When the first touch of daylight slipped in through the hole in the roof, I spotted a big fishing rod propped up in the corner.

So I thought, how hard can it be to catch fish?

I'll tell you exactly how hard:

hard

hard

hard

hard

hard.

The only bait I could see was one leftover potato in the bottom of the pan. I did think about eating the potato myself.

It turns out that would have been a better idea.

I looked into the water from the end of the jetty. There were streaks of sunlight under the surface like the shreds of orange peel in marmalade. Tasty-looking brown fish nosed right up to the potato, then turned around and swam away.

I don't know what the scientific name for these little brown fish is, but I decided to call them 'ungrateful fish'.

I wondered if the fish further out would be less ungrateful.

I stepped off the jetty on to the first rock. Hopped from there on to the second, just like Ryland had done. I got quite a long way out by rock-hopping.

The water looked colder and darker and deep.

But there was something there.

A big white wobbly square like a floating tablecloth or an underwater ghost. It got smaller, then bigger, which I realized meant it was dipping down into the depths, then rising up.

It was a big fish, or – as I liked to think of it – a big breakfast.

That is a good swap for one potato, I thought.

I dropped the line into the water just above its head, trying to find the fish's mouth. Then the whole shape vanished. Then everything went black.

One minute I was standing on a rock. The next I was being dragged through the waves and out to sea.

The big white tablecloth was not a big white fish.

The big white tablecloth was just one part of an *absolutely colossal* fish.

And the absolutely colossal fish had closed its big white mouth around my potato and the fishing line. It

had decided on a potato starter with a main course of me.

I was now the big breakfast.

The shock of cold seawater froze my brain, so my hands didn't think about letting go of the fishing rod until we were way out to sea. When I did let go, I had one happy moment where I thought I would bobble back to the surface and swim back to the jetty.

Wrong.

I surfaced, but the salty water was up my nose and I couldn't breathe. The spray was blinding my eyes.

My hand hit something slippy and surprisingly cold.

It was the side of the giant fish.

At least if I was holding on to her, she couldn't eat me.

She wasn't moving fast. Just kind of stealthily drifting along on the surface. I tried levering myself clear of the water. Up ahead I could see a dark triangle.

I tried to shout. Water swirled into my mouth. I got my head clear again, and that's when my brain realized the triangle was a fin.

Like the ones that sharks have.

I was clinging on to a shark.

A big shark – a very big shark. A shark the size of a bus.

The shark had barnacles all along her side. I tried to wedge my fingers in between them as she headed off into deeper water towards the mainland. I could even hear the church bells ringing. I thought she was going to take me right back there. Pretty stylish floating into the harbour on the back of a massive shark, eh?

But the shark had other ideas.

She veered off, carving a huge slow circle in the water until we were facing the island again. Now I had an excellent view of the island, but I couldn't really appreciate it because I'd noticed something over to my left. And over to my right.

More triangular fins.

Mine was not the only shark in the sea.

Sharks were on either side of me, all heading back towards the bay in perfect unison like something from

Strictly Sharks Ballroom. One of them flipped its tail out of the water and smashed it down again, as if to say, *I have a tail the size of a truck, so I get first bite.*

AranOr island was there in front of me, like Google Earth 3D.

There was the jetty.

There were the rocks.

The green hill rose up behind them. There was a dark fringe along the top, which I knew was the woods. I could see a thin grey scribble of smoke from our fire. As we got nearer, I could even hear Lola trying to get the others to tidy up.

The sea was very still. Suddenly what looked like tiny silver slivers shot clear out of the water and splashed back again just ahead of us. It sounded like applause, as though the sea was appreciating the shark-dancing.

I wanted to let go, but I couldn't. I don't know if it was my brain that was frozen or my fingers.

I shouted for help.

I shouted a lot.

The others must have heard me, but it was Eve who came running.

The shark and I sailed along the line of the beach and past the Big Black Rocks.

Even though I was about to be eaten, it was still interesting and surprising to discover another little bay just around the corner from ours.

Eve and Dario were now climbing over the rocks, trying to keep pace with me.

Dario was shouting something, but the breeze blew his words to pieces. When the wind dropped, I heard, 'BASKING SHARK!'

Seriously?

Dario thought I was interested in what species of shark was about to eat me.

'It's VEGETARIAN!' Dario was yelling. 'It's harmless!'

OK, the shark might be a vegetarian, but did it know I wasn't a vegetable?

The shark suddenly hoisted herself right out of the water. For a second I was sitting on a flying shark. Then all at once, I wasn't.

The shark belly-flopped into the waves.

The whole sea rocked and almost swallowed me. I saw the huge spooky white mouth ghosting towards me through the water.

I paddled like mad for the surface and hit my head on something hollow. Whatever it was bobbed out of my way, and when I finally got my head out of the waves, I saw it was the shocking-pink roof box that the drone had delivered by mistake.

Eve told me later that it was Ryland's idea to throw it into the sea to try and save me. Apparently saving each other through teamwork is something they do in *DogFight Rock* when they're not eating each other.

I climbed out of the water.

The others came running down the sand to meet me. Ryland helped Eve drag the roof box on to the beach.

'Basking sharks jump out of the water to get rid of parasites,' said Dario. As if this was a helpful fact. 'It probably thought you were a big parasite.'

'Did you see –' exclaimed Ada – 'what the Wee Gem was doing?!'

Eve looked at me as if to say, *WHAT were you doing?*

I could've said, *To be honest, I was mostly nearly drowning while potentially being eaten alive.* But I remembered what you said about make-believe and magic, so instead I just shrugged and said, 'Shark Riding.' Then, as though it was something I liked to do most mornings before breakfast, I added, 'On my shark.'

Ada smiled and said, 'We knew you were magic, but we didn't know you were THAT magic.'

Then this rogue thing happened.

The pitter-patter of silver splashes that I'd seen at sea began again, in the bay. Not just once this time, but over and over, while the basking sharks passed back and forth across the mouth of the bay.

Ryland and Dario ran back down to take a closer look. They paddled into the shallows, laughing and kicking water at each other. The splashes sparkled more like silver than water. The sunlight made them into silhouettes, and the spray shone around them like a blaze of magic. They looked like they were paddling in sparklers.

When I got to the water, I saw that the silver stuff was fish. Tiny fish, barely the length of my finger. Millions of them – so many packed into every wave, it was like wading in silver soup.

'This looks like it's all the fish in the whole sea!' said Ada. 'What are they doing?'

'Running away from the sharks,' said Eve.

When Dario pointed out again that the sharks were vegetarian, she said, 'Maybe the fish don't know that.'

'Oh no – look!' sobbed Ada. 'We have to save them.'

A wave full of the little fishes had rolled up on to the beach and left the fish wriggling around on the sand. We all crouched down and started chucking and shovelling the stranded fish back into the water.

I said, 'Keep some for breakfast.'

'How could you even say that!' cried Ada. 'They're so wee.'

They were quite wee, but if you had enough of them, they might also be quite tasty, and after we'd finished saving most of them, we might be quite hungry.

So while the others scooped them back into the sea, I shovelled fistfuls into the pink roof box.

Then, out in the sea just beyond the mouth of the bay, something boomed. We all looked up.

There was nothing to be seen. Then something jumped clear of the water. It was like an inflated dolphin. Its sides were black and white. None of us needed Dario or the internet to tell us what it was.

It was a killer whale.

It slid out of the water and into the air with barely a splash. Another boom.

'There's two of them!'

'So the fish came here,' said Dario, 'to hide from the basking sharks, and the basking sharks came here to hide from the killer whales.'

'So Shark Bay,' said Eve, 'is now an all-you-can-eat buffet.'

'And if we don't get off this beach,' said Ryland, pointing to the waves, which were coming nearer and nearer and rolling higher and higher, 'we will be next on the menu.'

So we clambered over the rocks back to our beach.

It wasn't easy, especially because we were carrying a 250-litre roof box full of wriggling fish between us. When it got really tricky, Eve would boost me up on to a rock. Then I would lean down and give them my hand to help them up.

Thanks to teamwork, we got back to the fire. And thanks to more teamwork, we had a mighty good feed. I'll send you the menu when I get the chance.

Until then . . .

Please come and rescue us.

From,

Noah

Letter 2

To: Mr & Mrs Moriarty
35 Glenarm Terrace, Limavady

Dear Mum and Dad,

The fish were too small to fry, so we fixed up a kind
of trestle table out of the bits of broken table from the
cottage and spread them out so that they would cook
in the hot smoke from the fire.

Ryland wanted to know what
kind of fish they were.

Ada said they were teeny tiny fish.

Dario said that that was not a biologically accurate name, but we ended up calling them that anyway.

While we were setting it up, Eve asked me what I'd been eating.

'Nothing yet – why?'

'You smell of food.'

'What kind of food?'

'Garlic bread.'

'Garlic?'

Garlic! It was the white flowers I'd stuffed in my pocket yesterday. I remembered now – Granny picked them for the pasta sauce that time. The leaves were the most garlicky bit. We spread them over the teeny tiny fish, and we had garlic-smoked fish with potatoes that we dug up and baked in the cooler bit of the fire.

I don't know if it was the garlic, or the fact that the food had been snatched from the jaws of killer whales, but it was pretty good, to be honest.

Even Ada ate it. It was her the idea to go looking in the plot behind the cottage. She pointed out that if the potatoes had been planted in nice straight lines, then anything else growing in a nice straight line might be food too. That's how she found bunches of carrots.

So that morning we had a big brunch after all.

'St Anthony's,' said Lola, 'we are getting good at this.'

We had scraped the carrots and were eating them raw like sticks of orange rock. Lola said this made her feel like a rabbit. Which was funny because just then we noticed a bunch of rabbits watching us from the scrubby grass on top of the sand dunes.

'Those rabbits look angry,' said Ada. 'Maybe these carrots belong to them.'

'If we don't want the rabbits to be angry,' said Ryland, 'we could eat the rabbits instead of the carrots.'

Dario said a rabbit would be hard to catch.

Eve asked if any of us had done any hunting.

Ryland said he'd done loads of hunting. On *DogFight Rock*.

'Not rabbits though. Wild boar. And not slightly wild. Wild, wild. Crazy flesh-eating zombie boar.'

'Did you catch any?' asked Eve. She was wondering if the skills you used for catching video-game zombie boar could be used to catch Real World rabbits.

Ryland said he'd caught hundreds. Mostly by setting up ambushes. 'Being honest, I didn't like the idea of an ambush,' he said. 'But my tribe was like, *No, we need to eat wild boar and we have a plan.* The plan was that I would be the bait and let the zombie boar chase me into Rocky Gap – Rocky Gap is the main landmark on level three of *DogFight Rock*.

'Everyone said I should do it because I had dexterity

skills and also speed was one of my character attributes. Anyway, I ran. The boar ran after me. At Rocky Gap I could see my tribe waiting, and when I came past, they didn't ambush it. They just laughed while the wild boar killed me and ate me and they got all my weapons and my skill credits.'

'So,' said Ada. 'You're saying you're dead?'

'Only in-game. I had loads of spare lives. It cost me two spare lives to get back to my tribe though.'

'The people in your tribe sound horrible,' said Lola. 'You need to sack those people from your life.'

'Yeah. We'd definitely make a better team. We could call ourselves the Treasure Hunters.'

'And we could call this Treasure HQ,' said Lola.

Ryland said he wanted to stick to Sea View Cottage because it reminded him of the other Sea View Cottage.

'What other Sea View Cottage?'

'The Airbnb Dad used to take us to in Portrush.'

That made me remember the time we went to Portrush and stayed in that caravan. Turned out everyone had been on holiday to Portrush at some point. Ryland said that Portrush was better than *DogFight Rock* and so was this place. Even the food. When he said that, the rabbits all scampered away.

If you're edible in this life, it's important to learn to move fast.

*

Maybe it was all the talk about holidays, but somehow my attempts to find the internet box that afternoon mostly involved paddling about in the waves.

Ryland got to work on a sandcastle, and one by one we all joined in, adding towers and turrets and moats. Then we all sat and waited for the tide to come in so we could see them fill up with water.

We lazed around in the sun all afternoon, watching little birds poking the sand with their bills or flying in and out of the rocks.

Dario tried to remember what kind of birds they were, but he couldn't.

Ryland said they were just 'normal birds', as though there were two kinds of bird in the World – gannets and normal birds. But really there were all kinds of different birds. Small birds with long legs that ran up and down in front of the waves. Big birds with curving beaks that seemed to stand still for ages. Tiny birds that sprinted between the rocks.

Ada made up names for them all. The ones with long legs she called Stilts, the ones with curved beaks she called Watchers, and the ones that went dashing around she called Sprinters.

There were different kinds of shells too. Some were shaped like tiny fans. Ada called them Tiny Fans. Others were striped and twisted like helter-skelters.

She called them wee Helter-Skelters. There were blue-black ones that were closed shut like purses. She called them Sea Purses.

When it started to turn cold, we all walked back to the cottage, laughing and joking, making up more names for places and things. I won't write them all down here. I've put them on the map so you can see them when we see each other again.

We found a big boulder that was shaped like a huge armchair and sat on it watching the sun go down. The hills in the distance seemed to disappear like clouds, but the clouds turned into massive red mountains in the sky. 'That,' said Ryland, 'is truly lit.'

We named the big boulder Sunset Seat. I wrote that on the map and just before it got dark, I renamed the island too. I crossed out 'AranOr' and wrote 'Our Island' in its place.

On the journey over, the others didn't notice anything, and hardly anyone talked or laughed. They were all too busy looking at their phones and scrolling through their feeds. Now everyone was seeing everything, and everyone was talking and laughing.

Maybe Dad was right about how it was easier to be happy when there was no internet.

Tonight Lola made us say night prayers.

No one could think of a prayer that we all knew

except for the *Our Father*, so we said that, but changed 'lead us not into temptation' to '*lead us to the treasure*'. And Ryland added, 'And don't let us get eaten by sharks.'

Someone added, 'Or rabbits,' and everyone laughed, and the hammock swayed as if it was laughing too.

I'm writing this under the hole in the roof, but it's not cold tonight, and the moon is so yellow, it looks like a big yellow cheese.

Don't worry too much about us.

Night for now.

From,

Noah

MONDAY

DAILY SPECIALS MENU*

STARTER:
Freddos & Choice of Crisps

MAIN:
Dish of the Day –
Granny's Magic Pasta
(Penne Pomodoro with Wild Garlic)

*Rabbits are off the menu

Letter 1

To: MUM
35 Glenarm Terrace, Limavady

Dear Mum,

I wish you were here.

I was so fast asleep that when it woke me up, I thought at first I was dreaming.

I heard the little bells again. Someone had picked up the phone in the phone box.

I slipped out of the hammock.

Outside I could smell the fire. Thick lazy puffs of smoke showed silver in the moonglow. I noticed something else in the moonglow. It looked like a pile of tiny white skulls. It was a clump of mushrooms, by the way. I'll probably try cooking them tomorrow.

I wasn't thinking about recipes just then. I was remembering that dark figure hunched up in the phone box.

I held my breath. I moved closer. Then nearly jumped out of my skin when someone touched me on the shoulder.

I spun around. 'Eve!'

'Why are you out of bed?' she hissed.

'Someone's in the phone box,' I whispered.

Eve took my hand and pulled me back into the doorway out of sight. 'SHHH!'

We waited.

Then jumped.

Someone touched both of us on the shoulders. It turned out to be Dario. 'What are you two doing?' he said.

'Someone's in the phone box,' said Eve. 'Making. A phone call.'

Dario tried to step forward to see, but Eve pulled him back.

'Wait,' she warned. 'Could be someone dangerous.'

Then another body pushed in between us. It was Ada. 'What is happening?'

'Someone,' whispered Dario, 'is in the phone box. Talking. On the phone.'

'Is it a bad person?'

'What's going on?' said Ryland.

Eve took charge. She pointed out – very quietly – that now there was more of us than them, and we all crept forward to surround the phone box.

Whoever was inside hadn't spotted us because they were still talking. Eve said to get our phone torches ready.

'Now!' said Eve.

The phone torches lit up the phone box.

A pale face floated inside the box, like a ghost looking out of a fish tank. Reflections of our own faces floated on the glass. The ghostly face opened its mouth really wide and screamed. We all opened our mouths really wide and screamed.

Except Eve, who quietly opened the door and said, 'Lola, come on out.' Because that's who it was inside the phone box. Lola. 'How are you making a phone call if the phone doesn't work without money?'

'It works for me,' said Lola. And as if she thought that sentence might not be enough of a surprise, she stuck a cherry on the top of it. 'I use it every night, to talk to my mum.'

That really was putting a cherry on top of the cherry.

There were a lot of questions, such as –

'Why didn't you tell us before?'

'Is your mum coming to rescue us?'

'Have you called the coastguard?'

'Will we get to go in a helicopter?'

Her answer to all these questions was, 'I don't know.'

'HOW CAN YOU NOT KNOW?!' we all said.

'Because I can't hear what she's saying,' said Lola. 'I just talk to her, and it eases my troubles, that's the thing.'

To be truthful, Lola's mum had not actually

answered the phone. Because Lola hadn't been able to make a real phone call. But she'd carried on talking to her mum as if the phone call was real anyway.

'What troubles?' asked Ryland. 'Apart from being marooned on an uninhabited island in the middle of the sea.'

'Do you think it's easy taking care of you all? Do you? Well it's not,' Lola snapped. 'Making sure you don't drown, or get lost, or eat more than your fair share, or forget to brush your teeth or say your prayers. And being in charge of the first-aid bag. It's hard work keeping you together while we wait to be rescued.

'And stop saying, *island in the middle of the sea*. ALL islands are in the middle of the sea.'

Lola tried to calm herself down. 'When things get stress at home, I just put a nice picture up on my feeds and let all the likes cheer me. Or I just write *I'm stressed* on my story, and people put uplifting comments underneath. I can't do that here. My phone won't work. It's so hard to be alone.'

'You're not alone,' said Ada. 'We're here and we like you. Don't we, everyone?' No one replied. 'I said, Don't we like Lola?'

The rest of us grunted. They were pretty positive grunts to be fair, given it was the wee small hours of the morning.

'There,' said Ada. 'Five likes.'

'Five's not many. I normally get fifty.'

'It's the entire population of the island.'

'Apart from the people who work in the massive warehouse,' said Ryland. Everyone stared at him. Had we somehow forgotten to tell him that the school trip was not going to plan? 'I mean it must be here somewhere?' he said.

'The fact is, there is one other person on the island,' said Dario. 'Mr Merriman.'

'I wish we knew where he was,' said Lola. 'I'm tired of being the grown-up.'

'Would anyone mind,' said Ada, 'if I had a go of the phone?'

Everyone seemed to think that talking into the silent phone was a good idea. Dario was already in there 'talking' to his mum. Ryland wanted to go next because there were things he needed to say that he didn't want other people to hear.

'I believe they can hear us,' said Ada, 'wherever they are. If we speak with all our hearts. Take St Anthony. He's been dead for hundreds of years and now lives in a different dimension – namely Heaven – but if you lose your door keys and ask him for help, he always helps you find them.'

'You're supposed to pay St Anthony if he finds your things,' said Lola. 'Well not pay him but give money to the poor.'

Everyone was talking at once because everyone was trying to ignore the fact that Ryland was speaking, not with all his heart, but with all his lungs.

'You left me alone. You promised! You tricked me! How would you like it if I did it to you?!'

'I thought he didn't want people to hear him,' said Lola.

'Woah, look up!' cried Ada.

Shooting stars were flickering across the top of the sky.

Have you seen them ever, Mum? They move so quick that by the time you shout, 'Look!' they've gone. But that didn't matter because there were so many, everyone saw one. It was epic.

'Little bits of space debris that burn up on entering the earth's atmosphere,' said Dario.

'Faeries,' said Ada.

Ryland leaned out of the phone box to get a better view and held up the big old black handset, the way you would if you were on FaceTime, so that the person on the other end could see.

'You know what,' he said into the phone, 'being stranded is actually OK.'

When Ryland came out of the phone box, everyone was staring at him.

'I feel loads better now,' he said. 'Thanks.'

Talking into the phone made everyone feel better.

Until we heard the phantom scream.

It wasn't a human sound. More like a deep growl or a groan, as if some huge hungry beast was getting ready to swallow us up.

I didn't even notice myself grabbing Eve's hand. I didn't notice us running back indoors. I did notice the back of my legs going cold with the fear.

Ryland and Dario pushed the cottage door hard back into its frame. I think it must have been them who shoved the cupboard against the window.

'It's the banshee,' said Ada. 'I'm sure of it.'

'What's the banshee?'

'It's the kind of spirit that howls in the night.'

It came again. Closer this time and less like a groan and more like something big and dead being dragged over gravel.

'Can it kill us?' asked Ryland.

'It's nearly frightened me to death already,' said Lola.

'They say you hear the banshee just before you die,' said Ada.

'*We're going to die??!*' said everyone.

Ada said she thought it would probably only be one of us.

Everyone shuddered. But I double-shuddered.

I looked at Ryland. He'd gone very white.

Banshee.

The last time I'd seen the word 'banshee', it was written on the bottom of the tide timetable up in the caravan. With a phone number next to it. Do murderous spirits have mobile phones? Do they stay in caravans?

Everything is confusing. Everything is frightening.

I feel smaller than ever.

From,

Noah

TO: Noah Moriarty
Sea View Cottage, AranOr

Oh, Noah,
Stop your worrying. Islands are full of noises. It says so in Shakespeare.

According to Granny, 'Fear is like a big seagull. You just have to let it fly over you because if you follow it round it will poo on your head.' No, I don't really know what it means either.

Look, you rode a shark! How could you be scared of a noise? You know Grannny's views on sharks? 'Don't curse God for inventing sharks. Thank him for not giving them wings!'

Isabella asked me to put her to bed early because she was worried that she might miss the next episode of her dream.

Granny made Yellow Man toffee, enough for the whole neighbourhood. That's all the news.

And, Noah – yes, you are small, but your big sister is seriously big. Stick close to her. No one is ever going to mess with Eve.

Dad

PS Dad was definitely not right about it being easier to be happy before the internet. We are not happy. Hurry up and fix. The internet.

Love,

Mum

Letter 2

To: Dad
35 Glenarm Terrace, Limavady

Hi Dad,

You said not to worry, and I don't want to worry you, but I was the one the banshee was howling about.

I'm in a fatal fix.

When I was writing before, I was mostly in Sea View Cottage with the others. Now I'm all alone.

How do the others sleep through everything, by the way? Maybe it's the fresh air. Maybe it's because they don't have to worry about saving the World. Anyways, I woke up because the phone was ringing.

This time, I got to the phone box in time to answer it. I must have only been half awake, because I was thinking it might be you.

It wasn't.

It was a voice shouting, *'We need an ambulance!'*

When I tried to explain that I didn't have an ambulance, the voice on the other end got raging. I did try to explain that they'd dialled the wrong number and were talking to a child who'd been marooned on an uninhabited island in the middle of the sea.

'*We need an ambulance*,' the man snapped, '*not a chat*.' And hung up.

Right away the phone rang again.

Someone else wanted an ambulance. I said, 'We seem to keep getting wrong numbers from people wanting ambulances, but we're just some kids on a school trip that's gone wrong. Could you help us? If you could ring—'

'*Sorry, mate. Troubles of my own*.' She hung up too.

Then the phone rang again, before I'd had a chance to leave.

This time I spoke first. 'We haven't got any ambulances. We haven't got anything apart from half a field of spuds.'

'*We don't need an ambulance*.'

'Oh. Right. Good. Sorry.'

'*We need the police and quick. Are you the police? Can you get here FAST? The situation is desperate*.'

'No. We're not the police. But . . . what's going on? What's happening?'

The man replied, but it wasn't the kind of reply I can write down in a family letter.

I looked across to the mainland, wondering why everyone suddenly seemed to need the emergency services. From over the sea, it all looked peaceful enough. The sun was just rising over the mountains like a big orange cake. The waves were smooth and still as jelly. But maybe sirens were wailing up and down Glenarm Terrace? Maybe there were riots and shortages all over those hills and towns?

No wonder Mum told me to hurry up.

If this was all my fault, then it was down to me to fix it. But how can you fix something so big when you're so little?

I made my way back to the cottage. I'd more or less decided to come right out and ask Eve to help me, when Ryland barged past me out of nowhere and woke up everyone in the cottage.

'Guess what I've got?!' he bellowed.

'A rabbit,' said Eve.

'A rabbit!' whooped Ryland. 'How did you know?'

'It's peeking out of your shirt,' said Eve.

'Yes. I caught a rabbit and it's THIS rabbit.'

Everyone bounced out of the hammocks.

Ryland opened his coat so they could take a look at the rabbit. They queued up to stroke it. They made cooing noises at it.

Lola went to fetch a carrot for it to eat. Ada started suggesting names for it.

The only person who remembered why we wanted to catch a rabbit was Eve. She said, 'You know we are supposed to be catching rabbits to eat them?

It doesn't need a name. It needs a recipe.'

'Are you trying to tell me,' said Ryland, 'to kill Buster?'

So the rabbit already had a name.

Dad, I want you to know that lovely as Buster the rabbit was, I stayed focused on saving the World. I really tried to get them back on task.

But it turns out that Ryland's rabbit was a bowl of ice cream drowning in chocolate sauce with sparklers sticking out of it. And me saving the World was a bowl of cold spinach.

No one was interested.

Ryland actually shushed me. 'Look,' he said. 'Buster has seen something.'

It's true. The rabbit's nose was quivering. Its ears were twitching. Its eyes were bulging.

Everyone followed Buster's gaze out of the window, out to sea.

The first thing we noticed was a whining noise. It was getting louder and louder. Then we saw something glittering and bouncing up and down on the waves. It was getting louder and bigger.

It was a boat.

A boat! A boat was heading for Our Island.

It was the same boat that brought us here. The same SkyHooks van was parked on the deck. Beanie Hat Man was standing next to it. And I could see a flash of fiery red hair in the little glass bit where the boat driver stands.

We ran down to the beach, waving and cheering, but instead of coming into the jetty, the boat veered off while it was still a long way out, turning towards Gannet Rock.

We ran over the sand and up on to the Big Black Rocks, waving and shouting. Which was pointless, as the boat's engine was so loud, the people on board were never going to hear us. As the rocks got higher, we lost sight of them, but we could still hear the boat.

So we ran up the hill and followed the noise along the clifftop.

Eventually Eve shouted, 'Everyone. Stop! Listen!'

We did stop and we did listen, but we couldn't hear anything.

'Exactly,' she said. 'The engine has stopped. They're somewhere down there.'

It was only when Dario noticed the two great muddy ruts in the ground that we realized where we were standing. We were right at the spot where the minibus had fallen off the cliff. Maybe the reason the boat engine had stopped was that the people on board had spotted the smouldering wreck of our minibus.

I took a step towards the edge.

'Noah, get back,' snapped Eve in her don't-answer-back voice.

I was amazed no one guessed that she was my big sister just then. They were all too busy thinking about the possibility of being rescued.

'Someone's got to go over there,' said Lola, nodding towards the edge. 'Otherwise they'll sail off again without rescuing us.'

Ryland pointed out that if they'd seen the wrecked minibus, they'd probably think we were all dead, 'and our bodies washed out to sea and eaten by sharks'.

'But if we wave to them, they'll come and get us, and we'll be home for tea,' said Lola.

No, no, no, my brain said. *You cannot leave until you've fixed what you broke.*

'But don't forget,' I said, waving the treasure map, 'we need to find the treasure first. Obviously.'

When I said that, Lola gave me a big sad smile. Then she looked at everyone else and said, 'We should tell him, shouldn't we? Wee Gem, *there is no treasure.*'

I didn't know what to say.

How did they know? How much did they know?

'Don't be sad,' Lola said. 'We just thought when you showed us that map, it would be a fun game to pretend we all believed in the treasure. We were worried about you, because you're so little. We thought it would keep your wee spirits up.'

'To be honest,' said Dario, 'I thought there might be treasure because, you know, the Armada and all that.'

If they didn't believe in the treasure, they wouldn't stay on the island.

If they wouldn't stay on the island, who would fix the internet?

I'd have to choose between being rescued and saving the World all on my own.

As they used to write on postcards – *Wish you were here*.

From,

Noah

PS There's nowhere to post this letter so I'll keep it safe for now.

Letter 3

To: Mum & Dad
35 Glenarm Terrace, Limavady

Dear Mum and Dad,

All the postcards of AranOr show the cliffs on the far side, the one facing the Atlantic. On the jetty side, you can see the mainland. Sometimes it drives you crazy how close it looks. You could be over the water and home in minutes if you just had a boat. It's almost cosy.

Cosy is not how I'd describe the clifftop. There really was nothing but ocean. And air. A lot of air. Because we were so frighteningly high up.

Everyone could see our best chance of being spotted was shouting over the edge of the cliff, but everyone could also see that it would be much better if someone else did this.

I was going to say something, but Eve broke in with one of those questions that she answered herself.

'So what are we going to do? This is what we're going to do.'

Eve got down on the ground and lay flat on her stomach.

'We have to attract their attention. But we don't have to fall off a cliff.'

She wriggled right up to the edge so just her head was over the clifftop.

'This way, you can see, but you can't fall.' Then she looked down. 'Oh –' she whispered – 'it IS high!'

We all did the same.

I was next to the muddy patch where the minibus had fallen.

I looked over the edge.

Put it like this, I was looking *down* on the birds flying. Not just normal birds. Gannets too. Their feathery backs were blinding white in the morning sun. One perched on the branch of a little tree that seemed to be growing straight out of the side of the cliff. The bird let itself flop back into the air, the way you might belly-flop into a swimming pool. It shook out its big wings and glided away.

I could see a little beach far below. There were towering black cliffs on either side of it, jutting out into the wide wild ocean.

I could hear Ada trying to think of a name for it. 'Look at those cliffs! Look at those waves! If you landed there, you'd never get out. You'd be stuck for all time. We could call it Sticky Bay. No, that's not good. Impregnable, that's it. Impregnable Bay.'

Way below, in the middle of the sandy beach, was a dark, tangled mess. A column of black smoke was still twisting into the air from one end of it, like a burning cake. Definitely, it was the school bus.

There was the boat, close into the shore, rocking up and down on the waves. Two people were on board. One of them pointed at the wreck of the minibus and maybe took a picture with her phone.

I tried to shout, but it's hard to shout if you're lying down.

Then all at once the boat's engine coughed. The boat skewed back into the waves.

They were leaving.

Without us!

I tried again to yell and wave.

Maybe that's what did it. Maybe the ground was dodgy where the bus had toppled over. Whatever. Somewhere underneath me, a rock came loose and bounced off down the cliff face. It crashed through the

181

tree. Sparks and blue smoke flew from the cliff face as it fell.

I tried waving again, thinking they'd notice the falling rock.

Then the ground just seemed to give up on being the ground.

It crumbled.

I fell.

Nearly every time someone falls off a crazy high cliff on to the rocks below, they are going to die a horrible death. So you're probably now thinking this letter was written by a ghost.

Maybe by the time you read this, I will be a ghost. That's if you ever read it. There's nowhere to post it.

But I'm not a ghost.

I did fall off the cliff, but I kind of fell in instalments. I'll explain later.

The main problem at the moment is that the others can't hear me calling from down here because of the waves. They also can't see me because they're too scared to look right over the edge.

I kind of thought Eve might.

But she didn't.

From,

Noah

PS I've just looked in what's left of the minibus. Some of it was still hot. I found a can of Irn-Bru, a party pack of crisps and a box of Freddos. Mr Merriman must have brought them with him as a treat or something. It's a holy miracle they didn't melt or blow up. It's good to have food. I might be here a while. Not sure how long a person can live on Irn-Bru and Freddos though.

PPS Something just happened. The sun slipped out from behind the clouds. All the nooks and crannies of the cliff look sharper. And now I can see a kind of cleft in the rock. It could lead to a cave – just a few feet up. Maybe there's tunnels. Maybe if I went in there, I'd come out the other side of the island. Or somewhere.

To be honest, going anywhere is better than staying here.

I'm going to find out.

I'm leaving this letter and my last one in the windscreen of the minibus, like a parking ticket, just in case I don't come back.

Wish me luck.

Noah

Letter 4

To: Mr & Mrs Moriarty
35 Glenarm Terrace, Limavady

Hi Mum and Dad,

Yes, it is me. Like I said, mostly when people fall off cliffs, they end up as human jam. So you're probably surprised to get another letter from me.

Not as surprised as the others were, though, when I ambushed them by the Pooka Pile.

I strolled up behind them, carrying a handful of Freddos and a multi-pack of crisps saying, 'Breakfast time!'

If this was a storybook, the others would have stood around me with bated breath, or whatever, waiting to hear the heroic tale of how I escaped from being hurled off the side of a cliff, with nothing below me but rocks and waves.

But this isn't a storybook.

Nobody's breath was bated.

Instead a major crisp dispute kicked off.

Lola opened the multi-pack and tried to make sure everyone got fair shares. Ryland was upset that she gave him prawn cocktail.

'Why are you giving me prawn cocktail!? Everyone knows I hate prawn cocktail.'

I did try to explain to them all how I'd landed in the wee tree that was sticking out of the side of the cliff, and how when I landed on it, my weight pulled it out of its crevice so that the whole tree fell off the cliff, with me stuck in its branches like a Christmas angel.

The only person who was impressed was Ada. And that was only because she thought I was now probably a ghost.

Eve pointed out that ghosts don't eat crisps.

'Oh,' said Ada. 'So he's alive!' She really couldn't hide her disappointment.

For the record, when the tree fell down the cliff with me in its branches, it landed on top of this kind of crag near the base of the cliff.

How did you get back up? asked literally no one.

'Where did you get the crisps?' asked literally everyone.

'They were in the back of the wreck of the minibus,' I said. 'And I got back by climbing up the cliff.'

Eve gave me one of her looks and said, 'Did you really scale a cliff with a multi-pack of crisps in one hand and a clutch of Freddos in the other?'

I would have answered her, but it was another of those questions that she wanted to answer herself.

'No,' she said, 'you didn't.'

That was true. I didn't. Not exactly. But I'll explain that later.

I've got something more exciting than the miracle of my survival to write down here. Which I also tried to tell them. Though when I said, 'I've got something amazing to show you,' Lola said, 'And we've got something amazing to show YOU.'

I pointed out that mine was definitely going to be more amazing.

She said no, because hers was really, truly amazing.

I followed them down a stony track that wound down to another cove.

This cove couldn't be more different. A bank of Furious Yellow sloped down to a wide beach where the waves rolled quietly up the white sand. There, drawn up on the beach, as peaceful as a pie left out to cool, was the boat.

I decided I'd name this place.

Paradise Cove.

'That's . . .' I began.

'The boat,' said Eve.

'Amazing,' I said.

'Amazing is right,' said Eve. 'This is our ride home.'

'But not as amazing,' I said, 'as this.'

The others had been so interested in crisps and chocolate, none of them had noticed that I was carrying something extremely heavy, slung over my shoulder.

I dropped it on to the sand and stood back so they could see what it was.

'Is that –' Dario gasped – 'what I think it is?'

'Depends,' I said, 'what you think it is.'

'That's the treasure!' said Ada.

'That,' said Ryland, 'is trouble.'

At the time, I thought Ada was right.

I now know that it was Ryland who got the right answer, first time. We are in trouble, a lot of serious trouble.

HELP!

Noah

Letter 5

Dear Mum and Dad,

I had to leave my last letter under one of the Pooka Pile stones.

I'll post it properly when I can. But I think a pile of stones that hasn't moved for a couple of thousand years is a pretty safe place to keep my letters for now.

To be fair, I didn't tell you about the treasure for a reason. I thought you'd really want to hear all about it and that would make you write back.

I really like hearing from you.

Maybe you have already written back. I don't know, because we are not in Sea View Cottage any more.

We are – as Ryland said – in trouble.

As if it wasn't bad enough that we got bus-wrecked, we are now sort of under siege. We're supposed to stay quiet and still while the kidnappers work out what to do with us.

The only good thing about being a hostage is that it gives me time to write and tell you all about the treasure.

The worst thing is, I think I know where the internet box is now, but there is nothing I can do about it.

I was telling you what happened when I fell off the cliff. I'd smashed on to the crag and was now perched on a tiny rock the size of a Colin the Caterpillar chocolate cake. But I was alive.

I lay looking up at the blue sky and the cliff towering above me. To be honest, I could have stayed there forever, looking anywhere but down.

My knees felt seasick. But when I finally twisted my head round, I could see it wasn't actually a sheer drop below the crag. A few feet down, it turned into a slope. A hard, rocky, steep slope. But definitely a slope, not a drop.

I nearly cried.

I could use the broken tree as a kind of ladder to clamber down.

My legs quivering, inch by inch, I shuffled towards the front edge of the crag. But as the tree tipped over the edge, one of the branches caught me and dragged me after it.

I tobogganed down the slope and on to the beach. Before I knew what was happening, my head was in the sand. If you're expecting to smash your head on a jagged rock, a pillow of warm white sand is a big treat. I snuggled my face into that sand as though it was a lovely, shaggy puppy.

I'd fallen just a few yards short of the wreck of the minibus. The front of the bus had concertinaed like a melted Viennetta. The windscreen was smashed. Its front wheels stuck out sideways like the fins of a fish. The back door swung in the breeze.

I searched through the debris of melted seats to find what was left of the bags. That's when I found the crisps and Freddos.

The sandwiches were not good to look at. They were covered in mould so hairy, it would have made Santa Claus a good beard.

There was a school notebook and pen, which is what I've been using to write these letters.

I was really hoping for a torch.

If the only way out of Impregnable Bay was a cave, then I really didn't want to try it in the dark.

There was no other way out.

The cliff was high and sheer – I know because I'd just fallen down it.

The rocks on either side jutted – sharp and dark – way out into the ocean. The waves crashed into them as though they had rolled there all the way across the Atlantic from America, getting bigger and faster with every mile until they were like great white hammers pounding against the crags. Which, come to think of it, they had.

Anyways, I didn't find a torch. Just one of those light-up screwdrivers, which gives you like a tiny measle of light. I took that and also a school hoody. It was too small for me – I think it's probably Lola's – but it felt warm and it reminded me of normal days at home.

I climbed up to that dark cleft in the rock. Inside the cave, it was totally dark.

My ankle snagged on something.

I pushed back all thoughts of the caravan ghost from my mind and felt around in the gloom.

It was string. Not exactly string, more like fishing line. It glowed when I shone the feeble light of the screwdriver on it. It was stretched tight and fastened to something behind me, which must mean that the other end was fastened to somewhere ahead of me. Someone had fastened it. Which must mean that it led to somewhere.

So I caught hold of it and followed it deeper into the darkness.

I'd gone about five paces, when I banged my head on the roof. The cave was getting smaller. I bent down. Banged my head again. Got on my hands and knees. I did not let go of the line. Had to admit that this was no longer a cave. It was more of a tunnel.

The floor was a kind of hard sand. Cold to touch.

The air was cold and really still. It was just hanging there. As if it was at a funeral. Like it had been waiting for you to breathe it in.

I ended up flat on my belly, with the roof grazing the back of my neck. To move I had to stretch my fingers and flex my toes, just kind of dragging myself across the stony floor, into the heart of the hill.

I thought about turning back.

I did try to shuffle back. It was harder than going forward.

The fishing line gave me a tiny bit hope.

It was just a piece of string, but it was all I had. *Some human had put it there. Some human had been this way before*, I kept reminding myself.

When I held that string, I was holding someone's hand in a way.

I stretched my hand as far as possible in front of me ready to pull myself forward again. Then, well, that's when the string slipped through my fingers.

I lost it. Or it lost me.

I was alone inside the hill, still as rock, like a fossil. I could nearly feel the weight of the hill above my head, pressing down on me.

I might as well have been in deepest, darkest space.

I stretched my arm further forward and felt around. The air on the back of my hand was colder. I tugged myself forward a little more. Then a little more.

Then I tried to raise my head.

I didn't hit anything.

I dug my fingers and toes into the sand, pulled with my fingers, pushed with my toes. Even though I couldn't see anything, I could feel I was out of the tunnel.

I tried – very carefully – to stand up.

OK, I was in a pitch-dark cave deep in the heart of the hill, but for a few seconds, the relief of being able to stand and breathe was amazing.

I stretched my arms out in front of me and tried to walk ahead. As I did, I dropped the electric screwdriver. It hit the floor with a clink and lit up. Not a measle of light this time, but a proper blossom of it.

It had two settings – useless and useful.

I picked it up and held it in front of me like a flower.

The cave was bigger than I'd thought. Its walls were curved and rippled. Beyond the curve was a splash of light.

LIGHT! There was a way out. Into daylight.

Honestly when I saw that, my chest swelled like dough rising. I walked towards the light, and that's when I discovered the treasures of AranOr.

An enormous pyramid of what looked like huge bars of chocolate wrapped in shiny foil. They glowed, as if they had their own light.

Gold.

Not gold coins like from the Spanish Armada, or gold rings like from a faerie tale. Just bars of nothing-but-gold.

Actual bars of actual gold.

I grabbed one. It's surprising how heavy a gold bar is. It nearly pulled my arm off. I wrapped it in the school hoody and tied up the sleeves so I could carry it like a bag over my shoulder and headed for the light.

The light was coming from a kind of slot in the cave wall quite high up. There were thick tree roots twisting all around it. So it was easy to swing up to but hard to wriggle out.

When I got my head out, the light was almost blinding. I had to wait while my eyes adjusted.

The first thing I saw was the Pooka Pile. I was right next to it.

D'you know what this means? It really was a treasure map! The X actually did mark the spot where the actual treasure really was actually buried.

Next to the Pooka Pile, there's this mighty tree. Its roots dig into the ground like it's looking for something. There's a gap between the roots where you can slide in and drop back down into the Treasure Cave.

You won't guess what I heard just then.

The terrible banshee. Twice. From somewhere close behind me.

I spun round.

Up on the ridge, silhouetted against the blue sky, was a big red stag. Its antlers were majestic. It stretched its head back, mouth wide open, and made the banshee groan. Except, right then, to me it sounded beautiful.

It was like the T-Rex roaring at the end of *Jurassic Park* movies, saying, *This is my island. This is its clean bright air. I am alive and so are you.*

When it finished, I wanted to stand up and clap. Write back soon.

From,

Noah

Letter 6

To: Mr Moriarty
35 Glenarm Terrace, Limavady

Dear Dad,

I bet you're thinking, *Woah, St Anthony really came good this time. He helped Noah find buried treasure that he wasn't even looking for.*

That is true, but if he'd helped me find the internet box instead, we wouldn't be in such a pickle.

Must go now.

Noah

PS You're supposed to give money to the poor if St Anthony of Padua helps you find something. How much would he expect you to give if you found a room full of gold bars, d'you think?

Letter 7

To: Ms Isabella
35 Glenarm Terrace, Limavady

Dear Baby Isabella,

Listen to this advice from your big brother. Don't ever find several million pounds' worth of gold. It's not worth it. And I'll tell you why.

There on the beach, with the sun pouring over it, the gold looked a bit like an unusually big block of luminous butter.

'Is that –' Dario gasped – 'what I think it is?'

'Depends,' I said, 'what you think it is.'

'I think,' said Dario, 'that is gold.'

'That's the treasure!' said Ada.

'That,' said Ryland, 'is trouble.'

'And that,' said Lola, 'is my hoody.'

As I said before, turns out Ryland was right. But I won't get into that just now.

'What,' said Eve, 'are you doing with a bar of gold?'

Ryland wanted to know how much a bar of gold was worth.

Dario said it depended on the currency markets, but usually it was a few hundred thousand pounds.

It felt heavy when I was carrying it, but I suppose it was quite light considering it's worth more than houses.

'I thought you said there was no treasure,' said Lola. 'I thought you said it was just a game to give us something to do and keep our spirits up.'

I pointed out that *I* never said that. *She* did.

'Hate to say this,' said Ada, 'but I'm disappointed.'

Everyone looked at her.

'I thought the treasure would be bracelets and goblets and crowns, not just a square brick.'

'The brick is made of gold.'

'Yes, but I'm nearly sure this is not faerie gold.'

'Unless the faeries have a brickworks,' said Eve.

Ada said that was dwarfs not faeries, and dwarfs were not real. But the gold is real.

Lola bent down to touch it, and Ada shouted to be careful because buried treasure is often cursed. The owners (for instance dwarfs) put curses on it to stop people (for instance us) running away with it.

Ryland said it's definitely true that gold is dangerous, and that whenever people find it, they always say they're going to share it, but they never do.

'How could we share it anyway,' said Dario. 'It's not a pizza. It's a piece of metal. It's a gold bar.'

Then I realized I hadn't told them the whole story.

'The thing is,' I said, 'the treasure isn't *a* gold bar. It's gold *bars*.'

They looked at me.

'You mean there's more?' said Eve. 'How much more?'

'About a cave full,' I said. 'Come and see.'

'Wait,' said Eve. 'You can't just leave a block of gold bullion lying around on the beach.'

'It's so heavy. I've already carried it all the way here. It'll be fine.'

Everyone had a go of lifting it. No one wanted to carry it. Eve said someone should stand guard over it and also keep an eye on the boat.

She didn't want to be that someone. She wanted to see the gold.

Everyone wanted to see the gold.

So we took it in turns to carry the gold brick back up the track to the Pooka Pile.

When we got there, Ryland said he wasn't bothered about territorial faeries, and moved a few stones around so that the gold brick was totally hidden inside the pile.

Then I showed them how to crawl in through the gap in the roots of the huge tree.

My first time in the Treasure Cave, I had to make do with a poky little light from the electric screwdriver. This time, four children turned on their phone torches.

Gold blazed out of the shadows like really expensive fire.

A lot of gold.

Dario said, 'Seventy-four.'

Everyone knew what he was talking about right away.

'Seventy-four gold bars at hundreds of thousands of pounds each,' whispered Lola. 'That makes . . .'

'Millions of pounds,' said Dario.

'Whoever lost this,' said Ryland, 'must be in trouble. I got a detention for losing a geography book. Imagine what you'd get for losing a pyramid of gold.'

'You know, now that I see it,' said Ada, 'millions of pounds in gold is not as disappointing as I thought it was.'

No one was disappointed in the gold.

They were so not disappointed that they wanted selfies with it.

Ryland made it look as though he was eating a gold bar.

Lola hoisted one bar over her head like a majorette with a million-pound pom-pom.

Eve shoved the bars around to make a throne of gold, then took a picture of herself sitting on it.

'Team photo,' said Lola, 'for school Facebook.'

'We don't have signal,' said Dario.

'But we'll have it one day, and then we'll be the school that found the treasure. Yay!'

When they ran out of ideas for pictures, they started talking about ideas for how they would spend a million pounds. Got to say, this was mostly food.

'No offence,' said Lola. 'But I'd give one of those gold bars for a fish supper.'

'With curry sauce.'

'And peas.'

'Salt-and-pepper chicken wings.'

I said, 'But you just all had Freddos.'

'I wasn't even hungry till I ate that Freddo,' said Lola.

When they ran out of food suggestions, they still didn't move. They stood shining their phones at the gold, making it sparkle and glow.

'What,' said Lola, 'happens now? I mean if you find a pile of gold, what happens to you?'

'Normally,' said Ryland, 'the finders team agrees to share it. Then they all fall out with each other and then kill each other, because, you know, greed. That's what happens on *DogFight Rock*. Every time.'

'Let's not do that,' said Ada.

We all agreed not to kill each other.

'I think,' said Lola, 'if you find a gold bar, it probably already belongs to someone. So we can't share it, because it's not ours.'

'Yeah, but finders keepers,' said Dario.

'I think finders keepers works for hair clips and biros,' said Eve. 'But not really for gold bullion in any quantity.'

'Not even on an uninhabited island?'

Then I said, 'But it's not uninhabited at the moment.'

'What do you mean?'

'Someone landed, remember. Two people. A man and a woman came in a—'

The BOAT!!! We'd all forgotten the boat.

We scrambled out the hole.

We legged it down to Paradise Cove.

We were too late.

There was no boat.

There was a trail of white foam in the water where

it had driven off through the waves. There was the buzz of an engine coming from somewhere beyond the rocks.

Any hope of getting off AranOr was sailing away.

We were on our own again.

We just stood staring out to sea. Maybe we thought that if we kept staring at the space where it used to be, the boat would somehow stop being gone.

Nobody said anything for ages.

Then Ryland said, 'I'm really hungry.' We knew what he was thinking. The bars of gold bullion looked just like huge bars of chocolate wrapped in gold foil. But they weren't chocolate. They were metal. Gold is all very nice, but you can't eat it.

We'd give a lot of gold for a fish supper right now. Or for one of Granny's soda breads straight from the oven.

Here's hoping we will all get to eat together again soon.

From,

Noah

PS Something amazing just happened. I spotted Eve holding what looked like an envelope in her hand. I asked her what it was. 'Oh,' she said, 'Yes. This came for you. I meant to give it to you earlier.'

A letter from home. Just when I needed cheering up. Thanks!

TO: Noah
Sea View Cottage, Island Of AranOr

Dear Noah,
You say you like getting my letters? Well you might not like this one.

What did you have to go and find gold for?!

The *ENTIRE POINT* of the treasure hunt was that there was *No Gold.*

The treasure hunt was just a cover for looking for the internet box.

Are you looking for that now? No you're not.

You even let a rescue boat go because everyone was too busy taking pictures of gold.

What did Ryland say? *Gold is trouble.*

It's true.

Gold changes everything.

Do you know what happened? I'll tell you what happened.

For thousands of years, this half of the World wasn't interested in the other half of the World. Nobody ever got a boat out to go and take a look to see if there really was anything over the ocean.

Until Hernán Cortés landed in Mexico.

Mexico turned out to be surprisingly full of people and roads and cities and pyramids. The people in Mexico were interested in Cortés's horses and his guns and his gunpowder. But Cortés was only interested in one thing.

Gold.

He used his horses, guns and gunpowder to get that gold, melt it down, put it on ships and send it home.

After that, the ocean was completely hopping with people, all looking for gold. There were fantastic stories about whole cities made of gold deep in the jungle, and kings and queens who washed in gold dust every morning.

Some people got lost and got poor. A lot of people got killed. The cities and the pyramids were ruined. The pirate Sir Francis Drake stole one treasure ship, and its cargo turned out to be worth more than England.

Everything changed.

All because someone found gold.

Gold doesn't change. It doesn't rust. It doesn't react with anything. It just sits there being gold. But it changes people into greedy monsters, burning cities, betraying friends, destroying everything. Even you.

Trust me. Forget about the gold.

Remember. Everyone is depending on you.

Love from,

Dad

Letter 8

To Whom It May Concern,

I am a Year Seven from St Anthony of Padua High School, Limavady.

I accidentally stowed away on a geography trip and got accidentally bus-wrecked with five Year Nines on the island of AranOr.

We are all now accidentally involved in a very, very big robbery.

I am writing this letter in case something happens to me.

To whoever finds this – we are not robbers on purpose.

We honestly didn't mean to steal millions of pounds in gold bullion.

It was an accident.

Yours truly,

Noah Moriarty

Letter 9

To: Mr & Mrs Moriarty
35 Glenarm Terrace, Limavady

Dear Mum and Dad,

I know you probably won't get this. But I want you to know that I did try. But doing the right thing somehow made things worse.

We all started walking back over to the jetty.

The little boat had totally disappeared from view. Beanie Hat Man and Fiery Hair Woman were probably back on the mainland now. Having their tea.

Lola's phone died first. They'd all spent too much time shining their torches at the gold. Ada's went next. Dario quickly turned his phone off, saying he had three per cent battery power left.

Then Ada said it was OK, because she had found a solar-powered phone charger in her coat pocket.

'You have a solar-powered battery charger,' said Eve, 'and you FORGOT TO TELL US?'

'That,' I said, 'is quite a big cake to leave in the oven.'

'Please,' said Ryland. 'Stop talking about food.'

They were so happy about being able to use a charger

that they forgot about being stranded. Everyone took turns charging their phones up and then wandering off the path to see if by any chance the people in the boat had somehow fixed the signal.

They hadn't.

Dario said it was probably good news that the people in the boat had gone away because now we wouldn't have to give them a share of the gold.

'Two extra people makes a big difference,' he said. 'Fifty million pounds divided by five is ten million pounds. Divided by seven is . . . a lot less.'

'Why seven?'

'Because they would want a share in return for taking us home.'

Got to say, a couple of million pounds in gold seems like a fierce price for a lift in a boat.

'And why five?' said Ryland. 'There's six of us.'

'Yes,' said Dario. 'But one of them is him –' he pointed at me – 'and he shouldn't even be here. He's not in our class.'

Eve pointed out that I was literally the one who actually found the gold. Which is true.

Dario said, 'Why are you always sticking up for him?'

'See?' said Ryland. 'It's started. People are dis-agreeing. Everyone will argue about the gold, and the next thing you know, some of us will be putting on war paint and building a fort. Why did there have to be treasure?! Everyone said there was no treasure. Why isn't there food instead of treasure?'

'The reason you're all arguing,' said Eve, 'is that you're hungry.'

She sounded just like you then, Mum. All the times when we had big arguments at home, it always turned out we just didn't have enough to eat.

I remember one time you said, 'Stop arguing. I'm going to make Granny's soda bread.' And you made soda bread in no time, out of stuff that was just there in the cupboard.

I said, 'Why don't we make soda bread like my granny. All you need is . . .'

I thought of all the things you need – flour, salt, sour milk. We didn't have any of them. Not even sour milk.

'Millions of pounds of gold,' I said, 'but no sour milk.'

'I want that soda bread more than all the gold in the World,' said Eve.

'We didn't know there was treasure,' said Lola. 'We thought it was a game.'

'Why go looking for treasure if you didn't want to find it though?' said Ada.

'Yes, why did we do that?' said Eve, looking straight at me. 'Go on, Noah. Tell them. Why did we do that?'

So I took a deep breath and told everyone the truth.

*

I knew it was going to cause trouble, but I had to do the right thing.

Didn't I?

From,

Noah

Letter 10

Dear Eve,

Seeing as we are not talking to each other, I'm going to write to you instead.

I'm sorry. I didn't mean to come on your school trip.

Love from,

Noah

Letter 11

To: My Dad
35 Glenarm Terrace, or wherever you are now
(if you've gone looking for me)

I really thought everyone was going to be shocked and furious, like Mum was when I broke that window playing football, but to start with, they didn't really even understand it.

They all thought the internet couldn't be broken. I tried to explain that the internet works through cables and router boxes, and they can all be broken.

Ada kept saying, *But the internet is in the cloud.*

I think she thought the Cloud was an actual cloud.

The Cloud is not actually a cloud.

So I pointed out some of the things that had happened since we got here – for instance, a plane that should have been flying across the Atlantic Ocean, flying so low it nearly gave us haircuts, and a pink roof box that was supposed to go to Germany being dropped through the roof of our cottage instead.

Lola said this could possibly be a good thing. 'My mum's always saying that the World would be a better place if there was no internet, anyway. She says people talked to each other more and, you know, it's true –

we've been talking to each other more.'

They finally started to worry a bit when Eve pointed out some of the things that might not be working without the internet, such as: Uber, Amazon, Google, YouTube, traffic lights, deliveries, electricity, banks, hospitals, schools. (Her list was longer than this, but you get the idea.)

Ada's mum is an Uber driver. Lola's works in a bank.

We were surprised to hear that Dario's gran has a YouTube channel about make-up. 'She doesn't even wear make-up in real life. She only does it for the likes and views. She'll get depressed, and it's all *your* fault. You broke the internet.'

'The whole World,' said Ryland, 'has probably turned into *DogFight Rock*, thanks to you. People all over the World are probably killing each other for scarce resources.'

Ada said, 'He used his magic against the internet.'

'He is not a magic child,' said Eve.

They all looked at her.

'He's a Year Seven. He stowed away on our geography trip. He's wearing our school uniform. He's just a little kid, and it's our job to look after him.'

Nobody was listening to her.

'The fact is,' said Dario, 'you need to find the internet box, locate the reset switch, and turn it off and turn it on again. It always works.'

'That's what I've been trying to DO!' I said. 'That's what the treasure hunt was all about. I wanted you to help me find the internet box, but I didn't want to tell you WHY, in case you got scared and panicky and ended up eating each other.'

'But if the treasure hunt was all pretend,' said Lola, 'why did you find treasure?'

'Because,' said Ada, 'he's magic.'

'He's *not* magic.' Eve was starting to sound cross.

'Excuse me,' said Ada. 'But if he's not magic, how come he's done so many magic things? He rode around on a shark. He fell off a cliff without hurting himself. He brought us food and gold. He even broke the internet. I mean, he seems pretty magic to me.'

'So what do you want me to do next?' I said. 'Magic a boat so we can all go home?'

I waved my hand towards the sea when I did this.

They all looked where I was pointing.

Then they looked at me.

Then they looked out to sea again.

Then their mouths fell open with surprise.

Because exactly where I had pointed, a boat was coming round the rocks.

'How,' said Eve, 'did you do that?!'

I shrugged. 'Magic.'

Because, well, what else was it?

*

We ran along the jetty and jumped up and down, waving our arms and yelling so that the boat wouldn't go by.

It was the same boat we'd seen earlier. Only now there was only one person in it, and as it got closer we saw that that the person was Mr Merriman.

It turned out that Mr Merriman had a whole menu of surprises lined up for us.

He tried to bring the boat alongside the jetty but kept bumping the front bit, which made the back bit swing out. In the end, we paddled out to it and climbed onto the platform. 'Like the man said,' Mr Merriman smiled, 'it's an easy boat to drive, but not to handle. It's like trying to sail a rocking horse. Now. What are you all doing here?'

The truthful answer would have been, *We were marooned after the teacher who was supposed to be looking after us – that's you, Sir – drove the school minibus off a cliff then disappeared.*

But no one said that. They were all just too happy at seeing a grown-up.

'Are you going to take us all home, Sir?' said Ryland.

'Yes,' said Mr Merriman. 'Just a few loose ends to tie up first.'

He waved us all on board the boat, and Lola started singing the St Anthony of Padua school song.

217

The boat see-sawed over the waves. For the first time in days, I felt as if everything was going to be OK.

Mr Merriman explained what had happened.

'I thought you'd all got a lift back with the ferrymen. I tried to call school to let them know what had happened, but while I was looking for a signal, I got lost along the clifftops. Then I saw the boat leaving. I thought you'd left me all alone on an uninhabited island in the middle of the sea.'

'The fact is, Sir,' said Ryland, 'all islands are in the middle of the sea, so there's no need to say an *island in the middle of the sea*.'

Mr Merriman smiled and said, 'You've obviously done a good job of looking after each other.'

No one was listening. Everyone was staring.

'What,' said Dario, 'is that?'

The boat had just come round the tip of the headland at Shark Bay.

We had never been beyond this point. A spine of jagged rocks jutted out into the sea. At the end stood a building, tall and white, shaped like a huge pepper mill with windows all around the top.

'Yes, what is that?' asked Mr Merriman. 'Anyone know?'

'The fact is,' said Dario, 'it's a lighthouse.'

'A lighthouse!' said Mr Merriman. 'That's it. A lighthouse. Very good.'

It made us all feel comfy and safe that he was still behaving as if he was on a school trip, instead of rescuing us from an uninhabited island. That's probably why we didn't ask him the really important questions like: *What's the right thing to do if you find fifty million pounds' worth of gold bullion under a tree, Sir?*

Instead, Ryland asked, 'How come we never saw the lighthouse before? Is it new?'

'Terrific question, Ryland,' said Mr Merriman. 'Who can answer that one?'

Dario explained that it was because the lighthouse was positioned to be seen from the sea, not from the island.

Eve asked him what happened to the people who came to the island. 'Isn't this their boat, Sir? Are they lending it to you?'

'Good question. Yes, but they don't really know they're lending it to us. At the moment.'

Mr Merriman had stopped the boat's motor and was bringing it alongside some steps cut into the rock where the lighthouse stood. He tied the boat up there and told us to follow him into the lighthouse.

As we climbed up the steps behind Mr Merriman, everyone was asking him questions. He wasn't listening. He pushed open the door.

Have you ever been inside a lighthouse? It was like being inside one of Ada's helter-skelter shells. The walls are covered with white tiles – smooth, shiny, curling around the corkscrewed staircase. That staircase seemed to want you to climb it.

'I couldn't find a signal,' Mr Merriman said, 'but I DID find this.'

He pointed to six gold bars stacked in a neat pile behind the door.

'Any questions?'

I realize now he was expecting us to be surprised by the gold.

We were surprised. But it wasn't the gold. It was the shelves that curved around the walls.

And on them was packets and boxes and jars and tins – of food.

'Sir, Sir,' said Ryland. 'Is that pasta, Sir?'

'Yes. That's pasta. And this is gold. Real gold.'

'And those tins . . . Are they tinned tomatoes?'

'Yes, YES, those are tomatoes. But getting back to the gold . . .'

'The little tins, Sir,' said Lola. 'Are they tuna?'

'Yes, the tins are tuna.'

'And this tin, Sir,' said Ada. 'Is it biscuits?'

She'd already taken the lid off and was looking inside.

'Yes,' said Mr Merriman, 'it is a box of biscuits. Correct. But we're not talking about biscuits now. We're talking about gold bullion.'

'But it's chocolate digestives,' said Ada.

Everyone was crowded round the tin.

'We can have chocolate digestives, can't we?'

'No, you cannot. You can't just stroll into someone's property and take their biscuits. It's one thing borrowing essential supplies. Quite another helping yourself to people's biscuits. Let's put the lid back on, shall we?' He put the lid back on.

We were all thinking, now we were back with Mr Merriman, he would know what to do and look after us, and everything would be OK again.

He did have a plan.

It just turned out that the plan was mostly not about rescuing us all from an uninhabited island. Mr Merriman wanted us to carry the gold bars from the lighthouse, down to the boat, and then take it back with us to the mainland.

Eve quickly noticed something was wrong with the plan.

'Sir,' she said, 'is this your gold?'

'Excellent question, Eve. Has anyone got an answer? This gold was just here behind the door when I arrived. Has anyone heard the phrase Finders Keepers?'

'We have heard it, Sir, but we don't think it applies to gold.'

'Interesting. Anyone else?'

'Are you saying, Sir,' said Lola, 'that we mustn't steal someone else's chocolate digestives. But it's OK to steal their gold bullion?'

Mr Merriman seemed to think hard about this moral question. When he'd thought it over, he said, 'OK, you can all have a biscuit.'

Everyone pounced on the biscuits. I have a feeling that Ryland got two.

Mr Merriman told us to grab one gold bar each and carry it down to the boat. 'Don't try to carry two. They're very heavy and the steps are slippy. Do it quickly. They will be looking for their boat by now.'

'Who will, Sir?' said Lola.

Mr Merriman said this was a great question and wanted to know if any of us had a good answer.

I said, 'The people who came this morning on the boat, Sir. They didn't come to fix the internet, did they, Sir?'

'Yes those people.'

'Is it,' I asked, 'their gold?'

'Excellent answer, whatever your name is. And what kind of people do you think might hide gold bars in a remote lighthouse?'

Dario suggested people from the Armada.

Ada suggested faeries.

Ryland said criminals.

'Criminals! Very good, Ryland.'

Lola said, 'Oh! I know what's happening now. The people who left the gold are robbers. Gold robbers. And now we're going to take their boat, so they're stuck here on the island, and tell the police all about them so that they can put them in jail and return the gold to the proper owners.'

'Very good, Lola – that's very nearly exactly right,' said Mr Merriman.

He said this in the sort of voice you might use for saying a Mars bar is nearly exactly a vegetable.

I said, 'So, why do we have to take the gold bars with us? Aren't the police going to collect them when they get the criminals?'

'We are taking the gold bars with us,' said Mr Merriman, very slowly, as if he was waiting for the rest of the sentence to be just right before taking it out of the oven, 'as samples. Samples of gold to show the police. Now grab one each, and let's load up the boat.'

If you're worried that me and Eve have accidentally become involved with a gang of gold robbers, and are going to end up in jail, well I'm worried about that too.

Write soon.

From,

Noah

Letter 12

Dear To Whom It May Concern,

It's me – Noah – again. Writing these letters as evidence. St Anthony of Padua High School geography group is innocent.

The Year Nines did help move some of the gold, but to be fair, if you go on any geography field trip, you expect to bring back specimens and souvenirs. If you go to the beach, you'll come back with shells. If you go to the forest, you come back with pine cones and acorns. So maybe Mr Merriman thought it was only to be expected that we'd come back with six bars of gold bullion.

There are two big problems with stealing gold.

One is that gold bars are much, much heavier than you think.

The other is that the person you are stealing it from probably really wants it back.

I was carrying one hefty bar down the steep and slippy steps when I heard shouting from across the water by the Big Black Rocks.

I guessed that was the bad criminals after their gold.

I also heard Mr Merriman. 'He's not coming quickly enough. We'll have to leave without him.'

'You can't leave a little boy on an island in the middle of the sea!' said Lola.

Dario reminded her that all islands are in the middle of the sea, but she said that wasn't the point.

'The point is, that this island is surrounded by sharks and has criminals on it. We can't leave him. That's not the St Anthony of Padua way.'

'The boy in question,' said Mr Merriman. 'Is he in my form group?'

'No, Sir.'

'So he's not my responsibility then.'

He started up the engine.

Eve stood up. The boat began to rocking horse again.

Everyone yelled at her to sit down and remember the sharks.

She stepped out of the boat. 'He's *my* responsibility. Because . . .' she said, '. . . he's my little brother.'

This was a big surprise to everyone.

'That,' said Dario, 'is rogue.'

No one was more surprised than I was.

I wanted to grab Eve's hand or say something nice, but Mr Merriman broke the mood. 'If he's your little brother,' he yelled, 'get him in the boat! Let's get out of here before –' he pointed at the rocks. Two people were picking their way across them towards us – 'THEY come and get us. *Come on*. Pass me the gold.'

I leaned forward, and Mr Merriman grabbed the gold from my hands as if he was starving and the gold was a hot pie.

Then I stepped back.

'What are you *doing*?! Just get in the boat!' he yelled.

I said, 'It's OK. You go. I'm not leaving. I'm not interested in the gold.'

Mr Merriman said, 'Excuse me?'

The others looked at each other.

I said, 'I broke the internet.'

Mr Merriman told me I was being ridiculous. 'The internet can't break,' he said.

'The fact is, it can be broken,' said Dario, 'and it has been. The link from the Midas Transatlantic Submarine Internet Cable has been disrupted. Oh! I just remembered its name. Midas. I keep remembering more things.'

'And now,' said Ryland, 'people are cowering in their houses, while cities burn. Our families are probably rooting through bins for food right now. All because of him.' He pointed at me.

'Yes. It's all my fault,' I said. 'But I think I can fix it. The big internet box must be somewhere on the island. If I can find it, I can fix it – and fix the World too. So I'm staying here until I've saved the World. Anyone who wants to can help. But that's what I'm doing.'

Eve stayed right by my side.

'St Anthony's – we'll fix the World! Yay!' Lola whooped. And she got off the boat and stood with us. 'Who wants to help Noah save the World instead of running off with a wee bit of old gold?'

One by one they all climbed off the boat and stood with me. They didn't even discuss it.

'Are you going to stay and help us, Mr Merriman?' said Lola.

'Errm,' said Mr Merriman, glancing at the rocks where the criminals were getting closer, louder and angrier.

'No, thanks.'

'But, Sir . . .'

Mr Merriman swung the bow of the boat out to sea.

'Help yourself to the biscuits!' he shouted.

And then he was gone.

I'd better go now. More later.
From,

Noah

Letter 13

To: The Moriarty Family
35 Glenarm Terrace, Limavady

Hi Mum and Dad,

'If you're going to do something amazing, make sure you eat properly first.'

I know that's what you always say.

We were planning to rescue the World from chaos, so – while the others watched in terror as bad criminals picked their way across the Rocks Like Teeth towards us – I nipped back into the lighthouse kitchen.

We were six children alone on an uninhabited island with some angry bullion thieves. 'Right,' I said. 'I'm going to make some tuna penne.'

I had pasta, tinned tomatoes and tuna. I found some olives in a bottle on the draining board. Threw them in too, and a handful of the wild garlic we found growing up alongside Our Waterfall.

I was hoping Granny's magic pasta would do the trick.

I figured out who they were right away. Their names were written on the tide timetable up at the caravan –

Spiky Jack and Mister Banshee. The men who'd brought us over to AranOr on the boat.

Mister Banshee must be Beanie Hat Man, because Spiky Jack was most definitely the one with the shock of spiky hair.

It wasn't hard to figure out who the woman was either. She was wearing a SkyHooks jacket with a name badge on it. Unlike the men, she hadn't taken her name off the badge. 'EMER: PROUD SKYHOOKS ENGINEER', it said. She also had a little enamel Aston Villa badge stuck on her overalls, just like on the key ring in the caravan. She was wee. More wee than me even. And her hair was blazing red like a crown.

They were raging when they burst in, but as soon as they smelt cooking, they slowed down and looked confused.

Food is like gold.

Food changes everything.

Mister Banshee said, 'What do you kids think you're doing?'

I said, 'Pomodoro penne with tuna and wild garlic, and some olives.'

'That,' snarled Emer, 'is *my* pasta.'

I said I was sorry, but I didn't know it was hers. 'We thought it belonged to the lighthouse keeper.'

'This lighthouse,' she snapped, 'has been an

unmanned automatic facility since 2004, when SkyHooks took over the island.'

'Why would an unmanned facility need pasta?' said Dario.

Mister Banshee tried to move the conversation on. He said they were shocked to find us here. 'We saw your minibus had fallen off the cliff and burned up,' he said. 'So we assumed you were dead.'

'Are they dead?' said Spiky Jack. 'Are they ghosts?'

'Ghosts,' I said, 'don't cook.'

'The main point is,' said Emer, 'you've stolen my pasta. And my boat. How are we going to get off the island without the *Skerryvore*?'

We didn't know what a *Skerryvore* was. It turned out to be the name of the boat.

Lola pointed out it was Mr Merriman who took the boat.

I said, 'Would a bowl of pasta help?'

Everyone stared at the pasta. They seemed to think if they looked hard enough, it would somehow get into their stomachs.

Emer said, 'No, a bowl of stolen pasta would *not* help.' For a second it looked like she was going to try and take it away. Our hearts stopped beating. But Spiky Jack said, 'Hungry,' in a voice like an earthquake and sat himself down at the table.

There was nearly enough to go round.

Mister Banshee seemed to feel he had to make up for Spiky Jack's lack of conversation by doing all the talking. (By the way, he said my pasta's tomato flavour was surprisingly intense, with a nice sticky quality. I told him that's what happens if you reduce the sauce, instead of trying to thicken it.) He wanted to know where I'd got the garlic.

Before I could answer, Emer said, 'Up by the waterfall. I used to play up there when I was wee.' She had a faraway look when she said that. 'It grew wild up there and thick as snow.'

It turns out Emer was born on AranOr. Her dad had been the lighthouse keeper, but when they brought the transatlantic submarine cable here, they offered everyone money to leave the island.

'I missed the place, though,' she said. 'That's why I

took the job with SkyHooks. Now I'm the woman who looks after the internet. Whenever I've a job to do, I stay over in the caravan.'

'Oh!' I said. 'So you've come to fix the internet?'

'When I'm in charge of something,' said Emer, 'it doesn't get broken. I take pride in my skills.'

'But the internet doesn't work,' said Eve.

'Because she turned it off,' said Spiky Jack, wiping tomato sauce from his mouth and pointing at Emer.

If a sentence could be a cake, that one was a three-tier show-stopping wedding cake sentence.

'You,' I said, 'turned it off?'

'Turned them both off.' Emer shrugged, fiddling with her Aston Villa badge as though it was a gold medal. 'There's always two cables in case one breaks down. It's called a *self-healing ring* . . .'

She probably told us a lot more technical information, but I wasn't listening. As soon as I heard that the broken internet was not my fault, it felt like someone had switched off the gravity in the room.

My heart was a sponge cake whose sponge was so light, it could float out of the oven.

I hadn't broken the internet after all.

The low-flying planes, the mis-guided delivery drone, the *DogFight Rock* chaos at home – none of that was my fault!

Nothing was my fault.

Eve looked even more surprised than me. She said, 'And you're going to turn it back on again now then?'

'When the time is right, we will.' Mister Banshee smiled. 'In the meantime, we apologize for any inconvenience.'

Suddenly, Spiky Jack stood up.

He was staring at the empty space behind the door where the six gold bricks used to be.

'Gold,' he said. 'Not there.'

'Our gold!' Mister Banshee growled. 'Where's our gold?!!'

'Oh,' said Lola. 'There was some gold there, yeah. Mr Merriman took it.'

'Who's Mr Merriman?!'

'He's our teacher.'

'Your teacher stole our gold! You stole the pasta. What kind of school is this? St Mafia's Academy?'

'We are St Anthony of Padua High School,' announced Lola with a sniff.

They weren't that interested in the real name of the school. Especially when Lola said that Mr Merriman hadn't exactly stolen the gold.

'He's more sort of borrowed it. There is more gold if you want it. It's in a cave . . .'

'We *know* where the rest of the gold is,' snapped Mister Banshee. 'We put it there. It belongs to big international bullion thieves. The six bars that were here were our little thank-you present for helping them. And now they've gone.'

'Go,' rumbled Spiky Jack. 'Go now. Everyone.'

He started shoving everyone out of the lighthouse.

I was the last one in the building. I'd begun stacking up the plates. Someone had to do the dishes, and somehow it's always the smallest. I don't think they realized I wasn't with them at first.

When everyone else was finally outside, I could hear a noise coming from somewhere up those twisting stairs. An electric buzzing noise. Exactly like the humming buzz I'd heard from the cables on the beach that first day.

Of course, what was it again? *'The safest, most weather-proof and earthquake-proof building on the island.'*

The lighthouse.

The big internet box with the on/off switch that I'd been looking for was up those spiral stairs. I started to climb them.

The noise got louder.

My heart was popping like popcorn I was so sure I was right. If I could just—

But then the mighty hand of Spiky Jack grabbed my collar, yanked me back down the stairs and pushed me towards the door.

'Don't forget this,' he rumbled, dropping the first-aid bag around my neck. 'You might need it.'

Got to go. Things a bit tense here at the moment.

From, Noah

Letter 14

To: Everyone at 35 Glenarm Terrace, Limavady

In case anything bad happens to me, I'll just say it now – thanks for everything, Mum and Dad. Especially for the letters.

They really kept me going.

This might be my last one to you. I'll make it good one. Like one last supper.

I had to get back to the lighthouse, but what could I do?

Mister Banshee and Spiky Jack marched us over the Rocks Like Teeth.

The sun was going down, but no one was watching the sunset.

I couldn't even look back at the lighthouse in case one of them noticed and got suspicious.

Emer kept looking out to sea, as if she thought her boat might be coming back. 'Where exactly did your teacher go off to in my boat?' she said.

Eve said she thought he'd probably gone home.

'But he's your teacher. You're his responsibility. He'll come back, surely?'

'Gold,' said Ryland, 'makes people forget their friends. And responsibilities.'

'The *Skerryvore*,' said Emer, still looking out to sea, 'was my father's boat and his father's before him. He stole my grandfather's boat. May his ghost drown him.'

'He stole our gold,' said Mister Banshee.

'I,' growled Spiky Jack, 'am annoyed.'

Spiky Jack pushed Dario aside and strode up the hill. He seemed to get bigger and more terrifying as he walked away.

Even Emer and Mister Banshee followed him in silence.

The SkyHooks van was parked just below the Pooka Pile.

Spiky Jack swung himself down into the cave between the roots of the great tree. We could hear him counting. A couple of times he got lost somewhere around thirty-five and had to start again.

We all just stood there listening.

Ryland seemed to think he was inside a game of *DogFight Rock*. 'This,' he said, 'is what we call a hostage situation.'

'No, no,' said Mister Banshee. 'We never said we were holding you hostage.'

'It's probably your best bet though,' said Ryland,

'because now six schoolkids know that you stole a load of gold. Their teacher has run off with your getaway vehicle. He's going to tell the police where you are. They're going to come to arrest you, and you'll have to negotiate with them. We're your bargaining chips.'

'Ryland,' said Lola, 'would you stop? This is not *Scooby Doo*.'

'I'm trying to help. They haven't thought it through. I'm trying to think it through for them.'

Just then Spiky Jack's head and shoulders erupted from the cave entrance. 'Anyone who sees that minibus thinks you're dead already,' he growled. 'No one is looking for you. It won't be hard to get rid of you.'

'Ryland,' Eve whispered, 'why do you keep feeding them ideas?'

'In *DogFight Rock*, it's all about the teams,' Ryland whispered back. 'If you can win people's trust or engage people's emotions, you can get them on your side.'

'The spiky guy,' said Eve, 'doesn't have emotions.'

'No,' said Ryland, 'but Emer does. We can get her on our team.'

'No whispering,' said Spiky Jack, finally climbing out of the cave. 'I don't like whispering.'

What he did seem to like was picking people up by the scruff of the neck and dropping them into the roof of the cave. He did it to all of us, one by one.

Mister Banshee lowered himself in after us and gave us our orders.

'Get all the gold in the van, then we'll drive down to the jetty, ring the coastguard. Tell them someone stole our boat. They'll come and rescue us and no one will know anything about the gold.'

'Because we won't tell,' said Ryland.

'That's right. You won't,' said Spiky Jack.

The cave was very, very quiet while we all thought about what he really meant.

It was Ryland who broke the silence.

'But there's no signal here, so if you're going to ring the coastguard,' said Ryland, 'you'll need to turn the internet on. But then our phones will start working, and because a lot of people have probably been looking for us, as soon as our phones work, they'll know where we are and come looking. Which will be awkward.'

'We're going to call the coastguard,' said Mister Banshee, 'on the landline.' He opened his hand and showed a fistful of coins. 'Emer here will stay behind and turn the internet on when we've gone. But now that you've mentioned your phones – good point, hand them over.'

'Nice work, Ryland,' growled Eve.

'Give me phones,' said Spiky Jack to everyone.

When everyone groaned and protested, Mister Banshee said that we should just hand them over or

Spiky Jack would feed us to the sharks.

'The fact is,' said Dario, 'the sharks around here are vegetarian.' Spiky Jack turned his gaze on Dario.'But here's my phone anyway.'

Ryland was next. 'Mine's broken,' said Ryland. 'It fell in the sea. I haven't got it any more.'

Spiky Jack turned him upside down just to be sure.

We'd already seen the gold twinkling in the sprinkling of phone torchlight. The gold by the light of Emer's proper engineer's torch looked different.

The torchlight seemed to turn on a glow deep inside the gold, the way sometimes lemon or salt or whatever will turn on new flavours in the thing you are cooking.

The brighter the golden bricks shone, the more they seemed to cast a spell on everyone. We all stood there staring at them.

Then Spiky Jack made us form a human chain.

We had to pass the gold along one brick at a time until each brick reached Mister Banshee at the top of the cave, who passed it up to Spiky Jack, who was waiting to put them in the SkyHooks van.

Because I was the smallest, I was at the beginning of the chain. Emer was positioned next to me, to keep an eye on me, she said.

'I think,' said Ada, 'the island wants us to be here. Think about it. We never set out to be here.' I think

Ada was just trying to make herself feel better. She carried on. 'And when we got here, the Wee Gem found us and magically rode around on sharks to bring us food. We are meant to be here. Something called us here.'

'Or some*one*,' said Lola. 'St Anthony, maybe.' Lola kind of glowed when she said that. 'St Anthony helps people find things, doesn't he . . . Maybe the *real* owners of the gold asked him to help, and he sent us here because we are St Anthony's. Yay!'

'My grandmother,' said Emer, 'Lord rest her soul, whenever St Anthony helped her find something, she used to put a piece of silver under his statue. In the front room. I can see it now.'

I said, 'According to my gran, you're supposed to give the money to the poor.'

'She WAS poor. She'd take the money back on the days when she was really, really poor.'

A thought dropped into my brain, like a coin dropping into a slot – the statue of St Anthony she was talking about . . . that must be the one we found in the cottage. So Sea View Cottage was Emer's granny's house. The E. McAlister on the letters was Emer's Granny.

Emer passed me another gold brick and said, 'I hear they call you the Wee Gem. Is that because you're wee, like me?'

'Yes. I get Wee Gem or sometimes the Hobbit.'

'Wee Gem isn't so bad,' she said. I think she smiled.

Ryland was right. Emer might be on our team.

When she turned away with her gold bar, I spotted something glimmering near the floor. The fishing line that I'd followed the day I found my way into the cave.

Something clicked in my brain.

I said, 'When you were wee and you lived on the island, I bet you played in here.'

'I did, aye,' she said, looking around at the swirling walls and up at the ceiling, which was a tangle of roots and rocks. 'No one even knew where this place was. It was just a rumour. Then I found it. It was my little secret hideaway.'

I didn't have to ask.

Emer found the cave because she was wee like me. Just like in *The Hobbit*. Why did those dwarfs take the hobbit with them all the way to the Misty Mountains? It was because he was wee enough to break in and steal the treasure from that massive dragon.

It was funny, we had a sort of a fellowship of our own. Me and Emer – we were the only two people ever on AranOr to know about the tunnel. The tunnel that led into the cave – and out.

Out.

That's when St Anthony maybe did step in, because Ryland suddenly gave a shocking great wail. Everyone looked round, thinking he'd dropped a gold bar on his toe or something.

'Buster,' he shouted. 'Buster is missing! Where is he?'

Straight away Mister Banshee wanted to know who Buster was. When he heard that it was Ryland's rabbit, he shouted at us to get on with it.

'The island is full of rabbits,' said Emer, kindly. 'We'll get you another rabbit.'

'But Buster is MY rabbit,' said Ryland. 'Everyone look for Buster.'

This was my chance.

Some people were arguing. Some were looking for Buster. No one was looking at me.

I stood with my back to the cave wall, near the spot where the tunnel was.

I dropped to my knees, felt around with my feet, and found the breeze on the back of my legs that told me I had found it.

Then Emer turned round and saw me.

I stayed, stuck to the spot, trying to think what I could say. But before I could say anything, she nodded her head at me. Just the tiniest nod, but it was enough. I pushed myself into the hole.

I inched into the rock.

I disappeared into the dark.

Behind me I could hear Spiky Jack's earthquake

voice rumbling, 'Get. To. Work.' All the other voices stopped. They were moving gold again. No one had noticed my disappearance. Or if they had, they didn't say anything.

It really was dark in there. So dark you can't even see the darkness. All I could see was the ghost shapes of the gold in my eyes, like when you shut your eyes after staring at a candle.

I lay there still.

The fishing line was just a piece of fishing line. All it did was show the way. But I held on to it as if it was pulling me out of there. I held on to it too tight. I must have tugged at it too hard. I felt it go slack in my hand. I'd pulled it off its hook.

I kept pushing forward thinking, *Just keep going.* But without the fishing line to guide me, there was no one to hold my hand. The cove was ahead of me. But something was holding me back, tugging at me.

I tried to bring my hands forward, but there wasn't room. Even the air seemed stuck. I wriggled sideways. Rock. The other way. More rock. I was wedged into some kind of little corner. I felt like I was being eaten. By the hill.

I tried to push myself backwards toward the cave, but the only part of me I could move was my feet. It's not easy trying to drag your whole body when there's no room to move. My heart was beating faster. It was getting hard to breathe.

And then something small and sharp and bristly skittered over my feet and brushed my ankles. Rats. Something warm and furry scratched at the back of my legs and scampered along my back. I screwed up my eyes. When I opened them again, maybe my eyes had adjusted to the darkness, or maybe there was the tiniest chink of light – whatever – something round and white was bobbling about in front of my face.

A rabbit's tail!

Buster!

There was a scratching sound and dust flying in my face, as if the rabbit was trying to dig his way through the rock. He wasn't. He was scrambling up it. I saw his tail disappearing up a slope.

Seeing Buster seemed to restart my brain.

Of course nothing had hold of my foot. The strap of the first-aid bag had snagged on a rock. I'd forgotten I was still wearing it. I had to shuffle forwards and backward to free it. Then I followed Buster up and out of the tunnel into the open air.

The sea was so bright, and wild, and furious after the darkness that at first I couldn't look at it, only listen to it. For some reason, I said, 'Hello.'

I looked down. Buster ran over my feet, then sat there, wrinkling his nose at the sea. So someone was looking after me. Even if that someone was a rabbit.

But I was going to need more than a rabbit for what I had to do next. To try and climb that cliff. Out of Impregnable Bay.

Goodbye.

From,

Noah

PS I'm going to put this under the back windscreen wiper of the minibus. I suppose if you're reading this, then you already know that.

MONDAY EVENING AND AFTER

AFTERS MENU

Mainly Tea & Biscuits
served at
Donegal Garda Síochána
&
Letterkenny Hospital

Porridge – Mess Tray Portions
Self-Service, Castlerea Prison

··

TWITTER FEED

@GardaSiochana Guards today arrested three people on AranOr island suspected of masterminding the so-called Belfast Bullion Bust Robbery.

··

@GardaSiochana The Guard also rescued five Limavady schoolchildren, believed to have been held hostage by the AranOr bullion gang.

··

MEMO FROM SGT MCCLUSKEY

A spokesperson from St Anthony of Padua
High School confirms only five children
missing. We have rescued five children.
One, namely Eve Moriarty, maintains
her little brother 'stowed away' on the
trip. The children agree there was indeed
another child, although Ada Adamski
suggests that the missing child is in
fact a magical being, who rides around on
basking sharks and led them to the buried
treasure. I did point out that it wouldn't
be usual for a child to bunk on to a school
trip. However, the trip's first-aid officer,
Lola Casement, was able to satisfy us that
the missing child did exist by showing us
a photograph of him on her phone. Being
honest, in the photograph the child in
question did appear to be riding a shark.

An abandoned vessel, the MV *Skerryvore*,
was recovered offshore by the Irish
Coastguard earlier this evening.

A teacher, Mr Merriman, remains at large.
Despite Mr Merriman's specialist subject
being geography, he appears to be lost.

The MV *Skerryvore*, locally known as the
lighthouse keeper's ferryboat, has been
impounded, subject to Ms Emer McAlister's
release.

249

INTERVIEW WITH EVE MORIARTY
Conducted by Sgt McCluskey

Please stop interviewing me and go
and look for Noah. He's very wee, even
for his age. He's probably in terrible
danger. He usually is. Stowing away on
school trips, falling off cliffs, riding
round on sharks. He fixed the internet.
He found your gold. The least you can
do is try and find him. I'm not saying
any more until you do.

Signed and Witness: *Eve Moriarty*

Witness: **Sgt McCluskey**

STATEMENT BY EMER MCALISTER
Taken by Sgt McCluskey,
Donegal Garda Síochána

I'm Emer McAlister, the SkyHooks
engineer who looks after the Midas
Transatlantic Submarine Internet
Cable connection on the island of
AranOr. I'm also captain of the service
boat MV *Skerryvore*.

I had no desire to be involved in the
robbery.

The big bullion robbers tried to
persuade me to help them by offering
me an enormous sum of money. When I
said I wasn't interested in money, they
tried to persuade me by offering to
burn my house down instead.

These fellas had heard there was a
heap of gold sitting in a warehouse in
Belfast International Airport, waiting
to be shipped to New York. Their plan
was to get me to switch off the internet
service to Ireland and the UK.

There would be chaos — flights
cancelled, traffic lights not working,

all the rest of it. During the chaos,
they'd steal the gold and drive it to
AranOr, it being an uninhabited island
in the middle of the sea.

I turned the internet off all right,
but when the robbers turned up with
the gold, didn't they have a busload of
school children with them.

Their geography teacher appeared
to have driven the school party over
the edge of a cliff. When it transpired
they were all still alive, there was a
heated debate about whether to turn the
internet back on again or not. First
they wanted it off, then they made me
turn it on again. Of course turning
it off and turning it on again made
the whole thing reboot, which meant
it turned itself off for a bit and
then . . . look, it's technical. When we
left the island the internet was off.

One of the kids — the littlest
one — somehow switched the internet
back on himself. We knew, because
suddenly there was a riot of WeeWord
notifications and alerts, and general
phone racket. The biggest robber —

Spiky Jack — got raging. He ran off to look for the kid.

Hope he never caught him. A little one like that wouldn't have much chance against the likes of Spiky Jack.

Anyways, it wasn't long before the Guards were here in boats, rescuing kids and arresting us. Which is fair enough, but I am totally innocent, as you can see.

What happened to the little fella? He sometimes goes by the name Wee Gem. D'you know?

Signed: Emer McAlister

Witness: Sgt McCluskey

Letter 1

To: The Moriarty Family
35 Glenarm Terrace, Limavady

Dear Mum and Dad and Baby Isabella,

I hope you'll get this letter.

I'm writing it because I want to tell you what Eve did.

I'm hiding just now.

Spiky Jack is after me.

Don't worry – my hiding place is probably the most hidden hiding place anyone's ever hidden in. He's never going to find me here. I don't think.

Anyway, I'm going to tell you what Eve did.

Remember I was in Impregnable Bay thinking about how to climb out? I stood there looking at that cliff. I couldn't see a way up. Even Buster the bunny couldn't climb that. But I had to find a way.

Remember when I fell from the edge of the cliff and landed on a kind of crag? I thought if I could get on top of that, I might see a way up the cliff from there. There were a few nooks and crannies in the rock and I got about ten feet up with no problem. But then I was stuck. I couldn't go any higher, and I couldn't actually see the nooks and crannies that I'd used, so I couldn't climb down. I thought about jumping down, but there were so many rocks at the bottom, I was bound to injure myself.

I could hear something moving on the other side of the crag. Something grunted. Some pebbles fell. You could tell it was something big. Being honest, it was a bit terrifying, hanging there on a rock face while some creature climbed closer and closer.

Then something hit me on the head.

And a voice shouted, 'Grab hold!'

I looked up.

There was Eve dangling a rope down to me from the top of the crag.

I said, 'Where did you come from?'

'I climbed up the other side. It's much easier. Always look before you climb. I looked in the boot of the minibus and found this tow rope. Here – give me your hand.'

Eve helped me up, but she wasn't happy. She said, 'I threw you the rope so that you could climb DOWN not UP. What are you playing at?'

'How did you get here?'

'I followed you through that tunnel.'

'But it's tiny. You wouldn't fit.'

'I did find that out.' She pointed to her legs and

arms. They were all cut and bleeding. So was her forehead. 'It was like being squeezed into a tube of Pringles,' she said.

When she saw me looking, she said, 'I'm your big sister. I look out for you.'

'You've spent the last few days pretending not to be my big sister.'

'I was angry with you,' she said. 'For crashing my trip. And for breaking the internet. Then it turned out you didn't break the internet. So I came to say sorry. And to stop you getting yourself in more trouble.'

It was nice – to have big sister Eve back. It was a pity I had to disappoint her so soon.

'I know how to fix the internet,' I said. 'Mum and Dad told me I had to save the World. In their letters. We have to go and fix it, otherwise what will happen to everyone? What will happen to us? We can't call for help until it's fixed.'

Then Eve said something that made me feel as if the cliff had fallen down right on top of me.

'Those letters,' she said, 'were from me.'

My brain went cold. 'What did you just say?'

'I wrote those letters.'

'So the letters I wrote to Mum and Dad . . .'

'Are here. In my pocket. They're all here. Even the ones you left tucked under the windscreen wiper of the minibus.'

'You lied to me.'

'To keep your spirits up. To tell you what to do.'

'You lied to me.'

'I was trying to make things easier for you.'

'You're all lying all the time. *Everyone* lies to me. Like saying we went to the food bank because we'd won a competition, and not because we had no money. I bet it's not even true that I ever have a bad touch when it comes to phones and stuff. I bet they only said that so they had an excuse not to give me one.'

To be fair, Eve looked a bit guilty when I said that.

'Look, Mum didn't lie,' she said. 'She just didn't want you to worry.'

'She said those tokens you have to get your food were the winning tickets. Like in *Charlie and the Chocolate Factory*.' I felt twisted up inside.

'That's not lying.' Eve sighed. 'That's spicing up the truth a bit to make it taste nicer. You know, like adding a bit of chilli.'

'Chilli is real,' I said. 'Winning a competition was made up.'

'But it *was* real. Mum and Dad made us feel like we were winning at life. They taught us to make a little bit of food into a feast.' She gave me a hard stare and said, 'Same as looking for the internet box and calling it a treasure hunt.'

Now it was my turn to look guilty. But if we were

going to have a chance of saving the World, we needed to move fast. Before the robbers noticed we were missing.

'Look,' I said. 'You went to the Cushendall Outward Bound thing. You know about climbing.'

'I know about climbing when there's crash mats and crash helmets and responsible adults. Not when there's rocks and wind and not a hint of a ledge or a handhold.'

Just as Eve said that, we heard this rogue groaning sound somewhere overhead. A stag was leaning out over the brink way above us, roaring into the wind. And then we saw it – about halfway between us and the top – a baby deer.

The little fawn looked like it was perched on thin air. But when the stag called, it took a step. And then another. The stag kept calling. The sun was sinking behind us. As the low rays of light hit the cliff, we could see – as if someone had marked it with a Sharpie – a series of cracks and ledges.

So there was *something* to stand on up there. The baby deer suddenly jumped from rock to rock, and next thing, it was up on the clifftop bouncing round its dad.

Eve said, 'Can a person follow a fawn up a cliff? No a person can't, because a person is not Rudolph the Red-Nosed Reindeer.'

I said, 'I got this far following a rabbit. I've got to do this.'

'OK, Noah,' she said. 'Lift your arms up.' She tied the rope around my chest. 'This is called a butterfly knot. I'm going to show you how to do it,' she said. 'From now on, it's not *you*. From now on, it's *us*.'

Sometimes the cliff bulged out so you had to duck to get past. It was easier for me, being so wee. After a bit we came to a cleft in the cliff. It was just about big enough for us to clamber into. It felt amazing to be somewhere even a little bit safe.

Eve said, 'This is a bit rogue, isn't it?' She untied the rope. 'A cosy little stop-off halfway up the cliff.'

When she said that, I realized it wasn't rogue at all. I'd made this hole. It was where the tree had been, the one I knocked out when I fell. We sat in there like two halves of an apple.

It seemed like nothing was rogue. I fell off a cliff, but a dead tree was there to save me. I knocked the dead tree out of its hole, and that hole was there when I needed it. Ryland catches a rabbit to eat. We don't eat it, and it saves my life. It was like everything had brought me here. Right back to when the minibus kidnapped me, and Lola's first-aid bag said I was 'NEEDED ON JOURNEY'. Because I was the only one small enough to find that tunnel. I was the only one small enough to save the World.

And exactly the same time I realized I was needed on

259

journey, I also realized I really could not face leaving the safety of that wee hole.

Eve knew without me having to tell her.

She said, 'Don't move. Don't try to follow me.'

'What are you doing?'

'Just trust me. Don't move.'

One of the normal birds flew up as though it wanted to get in there with us, then it tumbled away again. And Eve climbed out of the hole.

I don't know how long she was gone. I squirmed myself around so I was facing out of the hole. I thought if I could make myself look out, I might be able to step out. You could hear the waves battering the rocks even up here. Something dropped down next to me. It was the rope.

I could hear Eve's voice blown down from somewhere above me. She'd done it. She'd made it to the very top. 'Remember the knot I showed you?' she called. 'Use it to tie the rope on under your arms.'

I tied the knot.

'Stay in there. Let me pull it. Check that the knot holds.'

It did. She pulled me up off the floor and I swung out of the hole.

'OK, don't panic. Don't look down. Hold the knot. Lean back and walk up the cliff. I've got you. I'm your sister.'

I did as she said.

'Never look down. Look up. Look up and see me.'

I was not in any way tempted to look down.

I kept my eyes focused on Eve's head sticking out over the edge.

'That's it. Walk like Batman.' So I Batmanned up the cliff. Until Eve reached down and grabbed my hand and pulled me up on to the grass.

She put her arms around me. I put my arms round her.

I don't know how long we stayed like that. We were both tingling. Like electricity was running through us.

'You know what we are?' she said.

'What?'

'Alive.'

Yeah. We were alive. And being alive felt fizzing.

I just wanted to let you know. She's a really good big sister.

We ran all the way back down to the beach feeling like we could run forever. We only stopped when we saw something shining on the rocks. Ryland's phone. I put it in my pocket. I tried not to think about what might be happening to him and the others in the cave. Or what Spiky Jack would do when he finally noticed that me and Eve were missing.

I had everything worked out.

I explained to Eve.

'We've got to get to the cottage,' I said. 'There's a spare set of keys there. I saw the same keys on an Aston Villa key ring in the caravan. Then they disappeared. I thought it was ghost, but it was Emer. She's a Villa fan. They're *her* keys. She's the only real SkyHooks engineer. Those keys, they're not for the caravan. They don't fit the lighthouse door. There are no other buildings on AranOr. We've looked. They've got to be the keys to the big internet box.'

'What if they're not in the cottage any more?' said Eve.

'Why would they not be in the cottage any more?'

'Because,' she said, putting her hand in her pocket, 'I've got them.' She pulled out a key ring with two keys on it.

I said, 'Why have you got them?'

'The little silver one opens the post box. That's how I've been getting your letters.'

'That,' I said, 'is convenient. Let's go and save the World.'

By the way, this is the last piece of paper from the notebook.

From,

Noah

Letter 2

ARANOR LIGHTHOUSE KEEPER'S –
INCIDENT LOGBOOK

TO: Mum & Dad
35 Glenarm Terrace, Limavady

Dear Mum and Dad (also Granny Nuala),

Writing this on some pages I ripped out of a big fat book I found when I was up in the lighthouse. I think it was all right to take them. It was a kind of diary but no one has written anything in it since 2004. The lighthouse is lit by the way – not literally. But it is good.

At the top there's a kind of balcony with railings all around. That's where the light is – a great big glass ball with patterns on it. It looks like some kind of huge jellyfish.

When we arrived, there was a buzzing sound so deep it seemed to rattle your bones. It was coming from a big metal cupboard with a copper keyhole.

We'd found the internet box.

The copper key slid into that hole like a cake knife into sponge.

The door opened.

And there it all was. Wires, cables, chips, switches and red lights flashing on and off. All the things that let people talk to each other and send each other pictures across half a World.

There was a plastic flap labelled 'EMERGENCY RESET'.

I lifted the flap.

And there, underneath, was not a button . . . but a touchscreen.

'MIDAS TOUCH BIOMETRIC SECURITIES,' it said. 'FINGERPRINT ID ONLY.'

You could turn the internet on or off *with a fingerprint*.

'We've got to give it a go,' I said.

Eve put her finger on the Midas touchscreen.

It didn't work.

'It'll only work for Emer,' Eve said. 'Or someone with the same fingerprint as Emer. Which is no one in the World.'

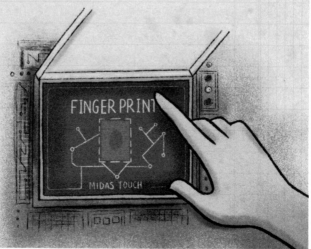

I put my hand out and touched the screen. Just for a moment.

The second I touched it, every red light stopped flashing. Then one by one they turned green. The buzzing sound got even louder.

'What did you do?' said Eve.

'I just,' I said, 'touched it.'

Something that sounded like a huge harp played a musical chord.

'Did I . . .'

'Fix the internet?'

I think I did.

'With your . . .'

'Yes.' I looked down at my hands.

'Noah,' said Eve, 'you fixed it. You are the reset button.'

It was really true.

No one else in the World could have turned the internet back on. It had to be me. The boy that the internet was allergic to.

Underneath our feet, the lighthouse rumbled. It was like standing on the shoulders of a giant with indigestion. There was a terrifying grinding noise behind our heads.

Eve covered her ears and yelled, 'Let's get out of here!'

I said, 'No. Wait . . .'

The lighthouse light lit up. We felt like we were dissolving in light. Down below, the sea switched from empty darkness to floodlit waves dancing as the light swept over it. And our shadows. You should have seen our shadows! They chased each other across the foam nearly to the mainland.

And on the mainland. Well, after the light had passed by, we could see, off in the distance, lights flickering into life all along the shores and roads. As though someone was painting a whole new country on the side of the evening. The warning lights of buoys by the harbour flashed on and off as if to say, *Come home. Come home.* As far as we could see, all the things that had been disconnected were joining together again.

We stood there watching, like two kids at a firework party.

'Now that,' said Eve, as the light swept by, 'is lit.'

Everything that was lost was being saved.

Then we heard something that sounded like a hundred tiny trumpets playing some kind of march. For a second I thought it was Ada's Faerie Army.

It was Ryland's phone buzzing away in my pocket. Its screen flashed endless alerts, notifications and challenges from his *DogFight Rock* group.

Then Eve said, 'The cave! I bet all our phones are ringing like mad!'

Which is when we both froze.

We'd each had the same thought at the same moment.

If this phone was working, then so were the robbers' phones.

What would they do?

Call the coastguard.

Lock the gold in van.

And what did Mister Banshee say? That everyone thinks we're already sleeping with the fishes.

Eve said, 'We need to call the police. Or the coastguard. Or Mum and Dad right NOW.'

She didn't sound like our Eve just then. The Eve that knows everything. The Eve that climbed the cliff face with her bare hands. She sounded like a scared little girl.

I looked at Ryland's phone.

'No good,' said Eve. 'We don't know his passcode.'

'BUT you can still make an emergency call,' I said.

I swiped the screen.

'NO – don't touch it!' yelled Eve.

Too late. It froze.

Devices really are allergic to me.

That's when we saw, on the far side of the Rocks Like Teeth, the gigantic shadow of Spiky Jack, stalking across the hillside in the lighthouse beam. His shadow was streaming towards us like a huge dark banner, as though he could grab us from a mile away.

He was coming.

Crossing the Rocks Like Teeth in the lighthouse light was hard. You had to wait until it swept back around again, every time it went dark. Up on the hill, the shadow of Spiky Jack stopped and seemed to stare.

I didn't have long. I'd told Eve to find somewhere to hide. Her legs were too bad to run any more.

I knew what I had to do.

I was going to ring the police.

I couldn't use Ryland's mobile.

But I could use the call box.

And yes, Dad. You're going to say I didn't have any money.

But – I knew where there might be some.

I ran all the way to Sea View Cottage. It was so dark I had to feel my way around to the mantelpiece. My fingers found the little statue of St Anthony. I said, 'Do not let me down now.' I'd remembered what Emer said about her granny always putting a few coins underneath the statue. I tilted it back.

There was a wee pile of coins underneath it.

I had the coins all ready to go into the slot in the phone box. Probably I should have phoned the police there and then, but I just really wanted to hear your voices.

I wanted someone to say, *It's OK, Noah. We'll sort this out.*

There, on top of the phone, was a folded piece of paper. The one that Mr Merriman had given everyone at the beginning of the trip. The one with the emergency numbers.

Eve had left it there the first day, when we couldn't use the phone.

I unfolded it. At the top it said 'IN CASE OF EMERGENCY'. Underneath it said 'Eve Moriarty' – and our home phone number.

So I rang it.

Baby Isabella answered.

I could just see her in my head, reaching up to take the phone down off the table.

'Baby Isabella,' I said. 'It's me! Noah!'

I could hear you, Dad, singing to yourself in the background. Sounded like you were busy in the kitchen. There was definitely cooking going on. I really wished that the phone had some kind of teleport option so I could just materialize in that kitchen.

I said, 'Baby Isabella, go and get Mum – quick.'

'Sorry,' she said. 'I'm afraid she can't come to the phone right now. She's doing a poo.' Then she hung up.

I stood there staring at the phone. I'd used up all the money. I put my hand on the receiver, thinking maybe somehow you'd ring back.

It was too late.

I ran up the hill.

I sloshed through the stream.

I kept on running.

I already knew where I was going to hide. I knew he'd never find me.

I'm still there now.

Granny, wherever you are, say a little prayer for me.

But not to St Anthony! Because someone is looking

for me – namely Spiky Jack – and I really don't want him to find me.

From,

Noah

PS I forgot to tell you were I am. I'm behind the waterfall! Remember the space behind the fall? There's a curtain of water between me and Spiky Jack, and he's never going to look behind it. I'm OK. But it's cold. I feel shivery.

PPS I just heard something. Like a howling sound. I know it's mad, but it made me think of what Ada said about the banshee and how you only hear her just before something terrible happens.

Letter 3

LETTERKENNY HOSPITAL, DONEGAL

FROM: PATIENT NO: (Don. 1786m)
Master Noah Moriarty,
Seamus Coleman Ward, Paediatrics, Enya Wing

TO: Eve Moriarty
35 Glenarm Terrace, Limavady

Dear Eve,

I probably should have thought that if a hiding place is too hidden for Spiky Jack to find me, it might be too hidden for anyone else to find me too.

I was saved by the banshee.

The wailing sound woke me up. And just in time. Apparently I'd fallen asleep. I'd got 'exposure', or something.

Anyways, you know what the noise was, don't you?

It was you.

You'd remembered about me having Ryland's

phone, and so when the Guards were looking for me, you'd got his mum and dad to use FindMyPhone.

And then they knew exactly where I was.

It was you who walked through the waterfall looking like something from a faerie story and yelled, 'He's here. He's fine!'

I said, 'I don't feel very fine.'

You said, 'I can't believe I've just saved your life and you're complaining already.'

The nurse here said, 'That's some big sister you've got there.'

Thought you might like to know that.

I also thought I ought to say thank you, Big Sister.

From,

Noah

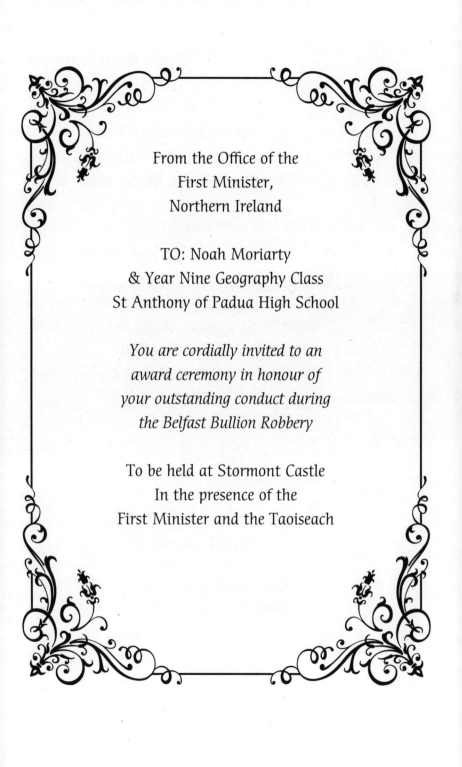

From the Office of the
First Minister,
Northern Ireland

TO: Noah Moriarty
& Year Nine Geography Class
St Anthony of Padua High School

You are cordially invited to an
award ceremony in honour of
your outstanding conduct during
the Belfast Bullion Robbery

To be held at Stormont Castle
In the presence of the
First Minister and the Taoiseach

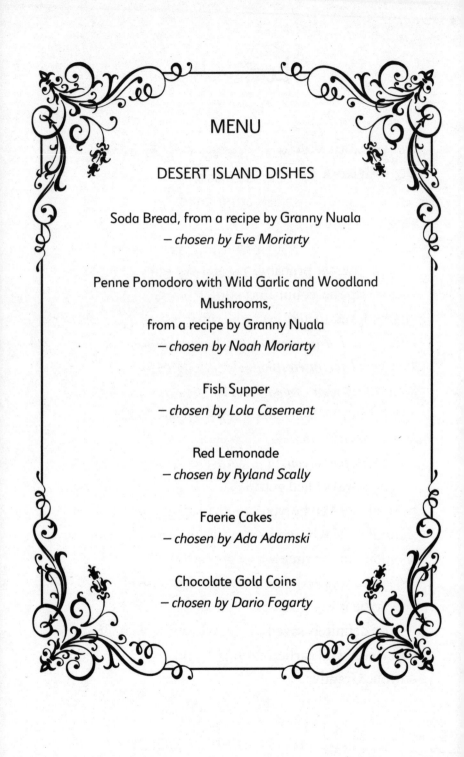

MENU

DESERT ISLAND DISHES

Soda Bread, from a recipe by Granny Nuala
— chosen by Eve Moriarty

Penne Pomodoro with Wild Garlic and Woodland
Mushrooms,
from a recipe by Granny Nuala
— chosen by Noah Moriarty

Fish Supper
— chosen by Lola Casement

Red Lemonade
— chosen by Ryland Scally

Faerie Cakes
— chosen by Ada Adamski

Chocolate Gold Coins
— chosen by Dario Fogarty

Letter 4

To: Granny Nuala
No. 9 Heaven or Thereabouts

Dear Granny,

I know there's probably no actual delivery to where you are up there, but I'm writing to you anyway.

Eve loves to tell everyone how, when you died, I said, '*But I was going to tell Granny about this recipe I've found for interesting things to do with mince.*' And Dad said, '*There won't be mince where she's gone.*' But Mum said, '*Tell her what you like, Noah. She'll have perfect hearing and eyesight now and all the time in the world to listen to you.*'

You always liked getting letters and cards when you were alive. Maybe you could read this one over my shoulder. Maybe you were always looking over my shoulder all the time we were away.

Someone was definitely looking after me.

Maybe it was you who sent Buster to me.

You definitely saved all our lives with that pomodoro pasta with wild garlic and tuna. Spiky Jack has nothing on you, Granny.

Remember the thing you'd say? '*If you find yourself in the wrong place, it might be because wolves have been praying for food*?' Well, by being in the wrong place for me, I somehow was in the right place for everyone else.

Anyways, you missed a grand time up at Stormont Castle.

We met a whole lot of important people.

Ryland brought his grandad with him – the one he plays *DogFight Rock* with. I saw him pocketing all the miniature Bounty bars from the buffet. That's when I gave Ryland his Switch back. It's a funny thing. He never did actually ask me for it. He probably got so caught up in the treasure hunt, that he forgot. He said it was a crying shame that they didn't let us keep the gold.

Being honest, it was a wee bit disappointing.

Lola brought her entire majorette troupe. They danced to a song called 'Golden Years' while waving gold pom-poms.

Emer was there too. She sailed herself over on the *Skerryvore*. She didn't go to jail, but she has to wear an electronic tag on her ankle in case she tries to leave the country.

Spiky Jack and Mister Banshee were not there. 'They,' said Emer, as she picked up her fish supper, 'are in jail. Eating nothing but porridge.'

Dario has been searching all over the internet for some clue to the mysterious fate of Mr Merriman. He says there's a cafe in Brazil called The Merry Man whose owner is the double of him. Ada said maybe he'd ended up paddling up the Orinoco River after all.

Basically if someone jumps into a ferry boat with a pile of gold, they're probably not going to turn up to school on Monday.

At school, Ms Gyngell is slightly jealous. Her class *definitely* are. Apparently the wonders of the Wonder Warehouse are nothing compared to being held hostage on an island with only crisps and chocolate for breakfast. They might be right.

The government thanked us for fixing the internet, ending all the chaos and rescuing the stolen gold – well, most of it. And a woman with a gold chain round her neck made a big speech about it being good to remember that there are things to be seen that are not on screens.

Which was definitely true. For instance, we talked more on AranOr. And we noticed things. Dario's been searching Wikipedia for the real names of all the plants and birds we named. Furious Yellow is really called gorse. The Rocks Like Teeth are called the Skerries. But being honest, I prefer our names. The ones we gave to the things on Our Island.

Being there with no phones was like going on

holiday to what the World was like when you were a little girl, Granny. But with extra gold bullion.

And when you think about it, you are further away than anyone, but here I am talking to you without a phone.

Anyways, as soon as the woman with the gold chain finished her speech, she called us up on to the stage and gave each of us a state-of-the-art mobile phone with the contracts paid as a reward.

Which is a wee bit of a contradiction.

The mightiest part of getting rescued from Our Island was definitely the helicopter. They wrapped me in one of those tin-foil blankets like a roast chicken and fed me hot chocolate until I started making sense. Then we took off – and guess what I saw?

The whole of Our Island from up above.

It was dark, but the helicopter carries a searchlight. It threw a bright yellow yolk of light across all the places we'd been – Our Waterfall, Sea View Cottage, Shark Bay – as it flew by. Like decorations on top of a birthday cake. I could see the little island, all alone in the sea, its cliffs and headlands reaching into the waves, as though it was trying to swim away. Except, it wasn't all alone. Not really.

There was the phone box that could carry your voice to anyone, anywhere in the World, even – if Ada is right about its reception – to Heaven.

There was the lighthouse, shining over the boats moving between harbours. And inside the lighthouse, I knew, was the internet box.

The magic box that lets people send messages, share memes, recipes, photos and memories.

Just then I was looking down on all the different ways, over the years, that people had been reaching out to each other. To say *Hello* – or *Goodbye*. From the first little boat that set out on the waves, to all the invisible messages zipping through an internet cable.

All of that had to go through AranOr.

People are like the internet.

If they don't all connect up – then everyone is in darkness.

Everyone is *Needed on Journey*.

Everyone is AranOr.

God bless, then,

Noah

NOAH'S GOLD WeeWord group

Noah Moriarty added you

Lola
Yay! Noah got a phone.

Ryland
It won't last long.

Eve
It's surprisingly Noah-proof.

Ada
Why is this group called Noah's Gold?
Have you found faerie treasure?

Noah
Just thinking about Our Island . . .

Dario
The fact is, it's not our island. It belonged to the
Marquess of Sligo, and then SkyHooks bought it.

Noah
Do you know, 999 CALLS ARE FREE? We could've
called the police from the phone box AT ANY TIME.

Ryland

I'm sort of glad we didn't.

Ada

The island was magical. Scary.
And cold. But magical.

Noah

I'm drawing a map, to help me remember.
Sharing it here. Did I miss anything?

Ryland

The devil birds.

Ada

The sunsets.

Dario

You can't put sunsets on a map.
Sunsets are temporary.

Ada

Temporary every night.

Eve

The wild garlic should be on there too.

Ryland

And rabbits.

Dario

What's the X for?

Eve

The X was always on there. It marked the spot where the treasure was. It really was a treasure map.

Dario

But the gold's all gone.

Eve

Has all the gold gone? No it hasn't.

Noah

Remember that first block of gold? The one we buried in the Pooka Pile?

Lola

So. There's still Noah's gold – on Our Island.

Eve

One rogue bar.

Ryland

Worth . . .

Dario

About half a million.

RYLAND SCALLY LEFT THE GROUP

Dario

Where did Ryland go?

DARIO FOGARTY LEFT THE GROUP

Lola

Where's Dario gone?

ADA ADAMSKI LEFT THE GROUP

LOLA CASEMENT LEFT THE GROUP

NOAH

HELLO ??

GRANNY'S SODA BREAD RECIPE

This is not a recipe. Making soda bread isn't just cooking. It's a life skill, like tying shoelaces or riding a bike. When the milk has gone off, you use it to make soda bread. When you're too late for the shops or you haven't any money, you can make a soda loaf, and everything will feel a bit better.

Quantities: Well now, I couldn't really just exactly say. You just get kind of a feel for it after a while, and of course it depends how much sour milk you've got.

INGREDIENTS
Half and half wholemeal and white flour – we'll say
    150g of each (you could use self-raising white if it
    makes you feel better)
1 teaspoon of salt
1 teaspoon of bicarbonate of soda (that's the magic)
Sour milk – about 300ml

METHOD
1. Mix up the flour, the bicarb, the salt and maybe a bit of butter, come to think of it.

2. Then pour in the sour milk. If you haven't got sour milk, you can make the milk sour with a drop of

lemon juice. Though that always seems a bit of a waste. Some of these young ones use yoghurt, and they say that works.

3. Pour the milk in there a bit at a time, and mix it in until you've got a nice dough.
Not too wet. Not too stiff.
Add more milk if it's too stiff.
Add more flour if it's too wet.
Knead it a bit but not too much.

4. Get yourself a nice round ball of lively dough.
Put it on a baking tray.
And cut a cross in it. Nice and deep. That helps it cook through.
Prick a tiny hole in the four corners. That helps the faeries fly out.

5. Bake at 220°C for about the half of an hour.
Take it out and pat it on the bottom. It should sound hollow. If it doesn't, stick it back in the oven for a wee while.

6. When it sounds hollow, put it on a wire rack to cool.

Whole thing takes no time and, at the end of it, you've a lovely loaf and a kitchen that smells of life.

AUTHOR'S NOTE

Although I made up the story in this book, a lot of the things that I made it out of are real and true.

For instance, my whole family really was once marooned on a small Scottish island with nothing to eat. It was only for one day, and we did discover a small packet of bourbon biscuits in someone's pocket, and we did get chips as soon as we were returned to the mainland. All the same . . .

It's also true – possibly – that there are some people to whom machines and devices are allergic. The Pauli effect is named after Wolfgang Pauli, the great Austrian scientist who was one of the pioneers of quantum physics.

Pauli was brilliant at formulating theories but terrible at experiments. Whenever he turned up in a lab, things would go wrong. His friend Otto Stern said that any experiment that happened when Pauli was near didn't count because he had such a bad effect on the equipment. In the end, Otto banned Pauli from his lab.

Everyone knew about this. So when a piece of very expensive equipment broke for no reason in a lab in Göttingen, the chief scientist there sent Pauli a funny message saying that at least this time it couldn't be

HIS fault. Pauli wrote back asking when the accident had happened. It turned out that at the exact moment the equipment broke, Pauli was changing trains in . . . Göttingen!

It's definitely true that we trust our satnavs more than we should. The rangers in Death Valley in California have a phrase for people who trust their satnavs too much and who end up stranded and starving in remote gulches when they thought they were going to Las Vegas. They call it 'death by GPS'.

If you want to know more about the amazing history of satnav, the whole story is in Greg Milner's wonderful book *Pinpoint*.

The internet has become so important to us so quickly that it seems like magic. It arrives in our houses as quietly as sunlight. It's like a huge invisible building that we all live inside.

But the internet is not magic and it's not invisible. We just don't know where to look for it. It travels around the world in wires and cables. Some of those cables are eight thousand miles long. In Shakespeare's play *A Midsummer Night's Dream*, the faerie Puck (whose Irish name might be Pooka) says, 'I'll put a girdle round about the earth in forty minutes.' That's what we've done. We've put girdles around the earth. These cables are real. They use energy, and they can be damaged.

I learned all about how the internet works from Andrew Blum, who wrote a wonderful book about it called *Tubes*. If you read that book, you will see that everything I say about the internet in this book is not quite true. Except the bit about sharks chewing submarine telecommunications cables. That really does happen.

The idea for the telephone that nobody answers comes partly from the beautiful 'wind phone' of Otsuchi in Japan – where people go to talk to friends and family they lost in the tsunami.

The idea for the not-really-a-treasure-map came from two places. Treasure Map was a game I played when I was about ten with a boy called Graham Fennel. We wove a cartographical fantasy around a big coal tip near our house. It also came from my son Joe, who made a film called *Treasure*, also about a fake treasure map. Strangely, Graham Fennel was the first person I ever wrote with. Joe is the person I sometimes write with now.

Yellow Man candy is also real. You can prove it by making some.

Writing a book is a bit like making Yellow Man. You take a lot of ingredients, mix them together, and hope for a little bit of magic at the last minute.

For me that bit of magic was deciding to set the story on an island. I got that idea from the children who visited All Write Now – a series of creative-writing classes I gave during the first COVID-19 lockdown.

We talked about how – because we couldn't go anywhere – we should practise imagining ourselves somewhere we really wanted to be. And I thought – why don't I do that too? So if you came to All Write Now, thank you. There are too many of you to name, but you know who you are.

Basking sharks are also real, by the way. You can see thirty-foot basking sharks idling around among the waves off the west coasts of Scotland and Ireland. I was lucky enough to see one in Mayo. Its open mouth really did look like an underwater ghost. The bit about waves full of tiny fish beaching themselves on the sand to escape from sharks is also true. There's a beautiful description of it in *Ring of Bright Water* by Gavin Maxwell, who used to fish for basking sharks.

Writing a book is very much like riding around on a basking shark. It's a very enjoyable and unusual experience, but there is no way that you are going to be able to steer it. You need someone on standby in case you get into deep water. That somebody is always my wonderful editor Sarah Dudman, who will jump into the stormiest waters and who knows the secret of shark-steering. And everything else.

The island in this book isn't quite real. It's a mixture of a real island off the coast of Donegal with some bits of story islands added in like herbs and spices to give it a bit of zing – islands like Treasure Island, Eye Land, Avalon, Gont, Craggy Island, Struay and Skerryvore (which is also the name of a real lighthouse).

I especially love the true story of some schoolboys from Nuku'alofa, in Tonga. They stole a boat and ran away to sea because they didn't like their school dinners. They were aiming for New Zealand but only got as far as a barren little isle called 'Ata. They lived there for fifteen months. Unlike in *DogFight Rock*, they did not kill each other. They survived because they looked after each other and learned to raise chickens. The whole cheering tale can be found in Rutger Bregman's book *Humankind*.

There are two really kind real humans whose names are in this book. They are Emily Gyngell and Isabella Watson-Gandy. A big Thank You to them for supporting two very special charities – Missio and Freedom from Torture.

The first person who ever whisked me away to a real enchanted island was my wife, Denise. Life has been enchanting us ever since.

ABOUT THE AUTHOR

Frank Cottrell-Boyce is an award-winning author and screenwriter. *Millions*, his debut children's novel, won the CILIP Carnegie Medal. He is also the author of *Chitty Chitty Bang Bang Flies Again*, *Cosmic*, *Framed*, *The Astounding Broccoli Boy* and *Runaway Robot*. His books have been shortlisted for a multitude of prizes, including the Guardian Children's Fiction Prize, the Whitbread Children's Fiction Award (now the Costa Book Award), the Roald Dahl Funny Prize and the Blue Peter Book Award.

Frank is a judge for the 500 Words competition and the BBC's *One Show* As You Write It competition. Alongwith Danny Boyle, he devised the Opening Ceremony for the London 2012 Olympics. He lives in Merseyside with his family.

ABOUT THE ILLUSTRATOR

Steven Lenton is a multi-award-winning illustrator, originally from Cheshire, now working from his studios in Brighton and London with his dog, Big Eared Bob. He has illustrated many children's books including *Head Kid* and *The Taylor Turbochaser* by David Baddiel, *The Hundred And One Dalmatians* adapted by Peter Bently, the Shifty McGifty and Slippery Sam series by Tracey Corderoy, and the Sainsbury's Prize-winning The Nothing To See Here Hotel series written by Steven Butler. He has illustrated two World Book Day titles and regularly appears at literary festivals and live events across the UK. Steven has his own Draw-along YouTube channel, showing how to draw a range of his characters. He has also written his own picture book *Princess Daisy and the Dragon* and the *Nincompoop Knights'* and his new young fiction series *Genie and Teeny*. For more info visit stevenlenton.com.